MY SISTER'S DAUGHTER

NETTA NEWBOUND

Junction Publishing

Copyright © 2018 by Netta Newbound

All rights reserved. No part of this publication may be reproduced, distributed or transmitted in any form or by any means, including photocopying, recording, or other electronic or mechanical methods, without the prior written permission of the publisher, except in the case of brief quotations embodied in critical reviews and certain other noncommercial uses permitted by copyright law. For permission requests, write to the publisher, addressed "Attention: Permissions Coordinator," at the address below.

Junction Publishing

United Kingdom - New Zealand

Junctionpublishing@outlook.com

www.junction-publishing.com

Publisher's Note: This is a work of fiction. Names, characters, places, and incidents are a product of the author's imagination. Locales and public names are sometimes used for atmospheric purposes. Any resemblance to actual people, living or dead, or to businesses, companies, events, institutions, or locales is completely coincidental.

Ordering Information:

Quantity sales. Special discounts are available on quantity purchases by corporations, associations, and others. For details, contact the "Special Sales Department" at the email address above.

My Sister's Daughter/ Netta Newbound. -- 1st ed.

For all my readers and loyal fans - Nik Plumley, Jackie Gerry, Livia Sbararo and Susan Foy to name but a few - thanks for the constant support x

PROLOGUE

I kicked the backside of the gibbering wreck scrambling up the stairs on all fours before me.

Watching with amusement, I followed behind him, to the large half landing, until he cried out, gripping his chest as though in agony. He fell onto his back, and one of his legs caught the hall table sending it flying. A huge vase filled with flowers clattered to the carpet.

"Oh, no you don't," I said, standing over the top of him. "You're not getting out of it that easy."

The knife sliced through the centre of his chest, gliding through the ribcage with ease and stopping only when the blade could go no further.

"Why?" he uttered. He slumped back as the life seeped from his watery blue eyes.

Expecting to have disturbed his wife, I waited—my senses on high alert as he took his final rasping breath. Then, stepping over the body, I clomped along the hallway to the master bedroom dragging my useless leg behind me.

I found her lying flat on her back, an eye mask askew on her pretty face.

Without hesitation, I grabbed her dark, curly hair and dragged her from the bed wanting to laugh when she almost swallowed her tongue in terror.

She screamed.

"Shut the fuck up!" I hissed, yanking her head back. An overpowering urge to bite her forehead, beside one delicately plucked eyebrow, was almost too strong to resist.

Kneeling beside the bed, she tore at the eye mask. Her face was a picture when she looked at me. She shook her head rapidly.

One slice across her throat, and it was all over. She flopped forward, a pool of crimson soaking the carpet all around her.

As stealthily as I could with a gammy leg, I made my way down the hallway, kicking open the next door I came to. I sneered and spat at the plaque in the centre of the door that said Princess Di. The messy room was empty.

"Bitch!" I roared.

I coughed to clear my throat before stepping back out into the hall.

DIANE WAS CURLED into a ball beside her father's desk in the downstairs office.

Her teeth chattered as she reached up to the desk and snatched the handset off the stand. With trembling fingers, she dialled 999.

She'd never been so petrified in her life.

"Emergency. Which service?"

"Help me, please," she whispered into the handset. A sound on the landing above her head made her whimper involuntarily, and she clamped her free hand over her mouth.

"Which service do you require, miss?"

"I don't know. Somebody has hurt my parents, and he's coming for me—please help."

"Help is on its way. Can you confirm your address for me, please?"

The stairs creaked one at a time, and her heart hammered in her chest.

"Are you there, miss?"

"Yes, yes. I'm still here, but he's coming. Please hurry." Diane ended the call and scrambled further under the desk, hardly breathing.

The door handle rattled before the door burst inwards with a wood-splitting crack.

She closed her eyes tight, not wanting to see the monster who had so savagely attacked her parents. She tried not to breathe, but she could hear her own rasping breath and knew he would too.

Another ear-splitting sound assaulted her ears, accompanied by the wail of approaching sirens.

CHAPTER 1

I SIGHED AND WIGGLED MY TOES IN THE SAND AS THE WAVES CREPT closer. The sun was setting, and the sky had turned a stunning bronze colour.

I loved Spain—had done since an early age when I used to holiday with my parents and baby sister in Cabo de Gata, a place just along the coast. Giles and I bought the villa seven years ago, but, each time I came, I ended up staying longer and longer. I'd been there for three months already and would need to think about getting back to my English home sometime soon.

Strolling back to the villa, sandals hooked over one finger, I relished the feel of the powdery yet silky sand under my feet. Then I climbed the steep wooden steps built among the rocks up to my veranda.

I would miss the solitude of Arenas Blancas when I eventually did go home. Unlike most coastal areas in Spain, Arenas Blancas hadn't been hammered by tourism yet. I had a scattering of friendly neighbours, who kept to themselves, and my lovely friend Angel. A far cry from my English home.

It was still too warm to eat dinner, so I opted instead for a plate of fresh fruit salad and settled down on the veranda. Dusk was my favourite time of the day by far. I smiled at the familiar sights and sounds I'd grown to love—waves kissing the shore, swallows making a final dart across the sky with their wings slashing through the still air, and the raucous squawk of squabbling seagulls fighting over their last meal of the day.

I didn't feel ready to trade it all in for the cacophony of sounds from the city just yet, but I knew I must.

I glanced at my phone and gasped. I'd been so wrapped up in my grief, I'd forgotten the date.

I dialled Angel's number—my dear friend and closest neighbour.

Angel was in her late sixties and she looked after the villa when I was away.

"Sorry to call you so late, Angel, but I've just realised I need to get back to England right away."

"Oh no!" The emotion in her strong Cockney accent brought tears to my eyes. "Is everything alright?"

I blinked several times and gulped down a huge lump. "I'm leaving for the airport shortly," I said, ignoring her question. I couldn't bear having to discuss it just yet. "Can I leave you to close up the house for me, please?"

"Of course, you can, lovey. Shall I ask Marvin to drive you to the airport?"

I hadn't thought that far ahead. "I need to go to Malaga as there's more chance of getting a cancellation. But it's too far for you, at this time of night."

"Nonsense. I insist."

"Okay then. If Marvin doesn't mind that would be great. Otherwise I'll make arrangements for parking. I don't know when I'll be back."

"What time will you be ready?"

"Thirty minutes? Is that okay?"

"We'll see you soon."

On auto pilot, I threw a number of items into my case. I didn't intend staying away forever, but I knew, once back in England, things would have a way of taking over even the best laid plans.

Angel and her trusted husband, Marvin, arrived shortly after. As soon as I set eyes on my lovely friend, I couldn't hold back the tears. I collapsed in a heap beside her on the sofa and handed her my phone.

Angel read it and then pulled me into her arms, smoothing down my blonde frizz. She muttered something soothing to me in Spanish.

Marvin carried my case to the car. I gave the place a final check and, linking arms with Angel, headed outside.

The three-hour drive to Malaga usually took my breath away, but we couldn't see anything of the spectacular coastal views I always loved. In fact I noticed very little, as I was lost in memories.

"Tell him how much I appreciate him doing this," I said, nodding at Marvin.

After forty-years in the country, Angel spoke fluent Spanish. She spoke quickly to her husband, who turned and smiled at me.

He was a man of very few words. I could count on one hand the times I'd heard him actually speak. Angel said she couldn't shut him up when they were home alone. I couldn't imagine it, however.

Angel nodded off to sleep in the front passenger seat leaving me alone with my thoughts.

We arrived at the airport at just after 2am. I insisted Angel and Marvin drop me off and leave, not wanting to cause them any further inconvenience.

I hugged them both tightly promising to call as soon as I could. Then I dragged my case inside praying I wouldn't have too long to wait.

The woman at the ticket desk booked me onto the next flight at 7.45am. Because of the late hour, I managed to score a daybed in a quiet part of the airport. I ordered a strong black coffee and sipped the bitter liquid hoping the caffeine would kick in.

CHAPTER 2

THE PLANE LANDED IN DRIZZLY MANCHESTER AT JUST BEFORE 10AM. I'd been able to spread out over a couple of seats and managed to get an hour's sleep.

Once through customs, I grabbed my case and headed to the taxi rank.

"Carlson Tower, Salford Quays, please," I said, climbing into the back of a taxi.

I felt as sick as a dog by the time we approached my apartment block. I rummaged in the bottom of my bag for some English money then paid the driver before getting out. "Keep the change," I called over my shoulder.

Taking the lift to my duplex penthouse apartment, a feeling of dread settled in the pit of my stomach. Not because of the place as such, but because of the memories the apartment evoked.

I let myself inside. The interior was a far cry from the quaint, ramshackle villa. It was stunning. Three double en suite bedrooms, a study, reading room, open-plan living areas overlooking the quays and the city of Manchester. I remembered how excited we were when we moved in. It was everything I'd ever dreamed of, but, without Giles, it meant nothing.

I threw my bags down and rushed up the flight of stairs directly in front of me stopping at the door at the far end of the landing.

Bracing myself at the door, I took several deep breaths before entering.

"Hey, my babies. Mummy's home."

CHAPTER 3

I woke to the incessant buzzing of the intercom and gasped when I remembered where I was. Manchester—home.

I slid out of the extravagant king-sized bed and pulled my silky pink robe from the bag beside the door.

The master bedroom was on the same level as the living areas, so I strolled to the intercom expecting to see security on the screen. I gasped at the sight of two uniformed police officers.

"Hello?" I asked, my voice croaky from sleep.

"Susanna Carmichael?" the young female officer asked, giving me an unflattering view up her nose.

"Yes. What appears to be the problem, officer?"

"May we come in? We need to speak to you in person."

"Hang on one minute." My heart thundered in my chest. *What the hell do the police want to speak to me about?*

I grabbed the bunch of keys from the hallstand and raced upstairs, along the landing, and with fumbling fingers locked the door.

Once I'd calmed my raging pulse sufficiently, I pasted a smile on my face and casually strolled back to the intercom.

"Come on up."

Moments later, I was seated opposite two young officers who looked as uncomfortable as I felt.

"What can I do for you?" I asked.

"We had a call from a Detective Inspector Conrad Jenkins from Carlisle Police Station," said the handsome young man.

My mind raced. Carlisle? Then prickles formed at the base of my neck and travelled down my entire body. My sister lived just outside of Carlisle. "What's that got to do with me?" My voice sounded much calmer than I felt.

"I'm sorry to be the bearer of tragic news, Ms Carmichael, but your sister and her husband were killed in the early hours of this morning."

I tried to make sense of his words. Steph and Eddie were dead? "How? I don't…" I shook my head in total confusion. "I'm sorry. I don't understand."

"All we know, at this stage, is somebody broke into their home during the night and attacked and killed them both. I'm so sorry to have to tell you like this, but the Detective was under the impression you were out of the country. We were asked to come by on the off chance you were home."

"I got back yesterday—I've been in Spain for three months."

"Yesterday?" the woman said, glancing at her colleague.

"Yes, that's right."

"Where were you last night, if you don't mind me asking?"

"Here—I never left once I arrived home. I hadn't had any sleep the night before, so I was shattered. Are you sure it was my sister? There's got to be some mistake." My heart ached, and I couldn't hold back the tears any longer.

"We haven't any more details for you I'm sorry. Here is the lead Detective's phone number." He placed the small blue post-it note down on the coffee table. "He'll be able to help you with any further questions. Would you like us to stay while you speak to him?"

I shook my head. "No. I'll be fine. Thank you."

They got to their feet, and I showed them to the door feeling as though I was stuck in some kind of terrible nightmare. *Who would want to hurt my beautiful sister?*

Trembling all over, I decided to take a shower before calling the Detective, still believing there must've been some kind of terrible mistake.

Afterwards, I found my phone and dialled the number the police officer had left.

"Conrad Jenkins," a gruff male voice said in my ear.

"Hi, Detective. I'm Susanna Carmichael. I've just had a visit from two police officers. Please tell me there's been a mistake."

"Ah, Ms Carmichael. I do apologise. I was told you were out of the country."

"I was until yesterday. Please, tell me what happened."

"A robbery by the looks of things. But it's still early days."

"I'm on my way. I need to be there."

"Of course. Let me know when you're in the area, and I'll arrange to meet you to explain everything. Hopefully, we'll have more to go on by then."

"Where's Diane?" I asked, suddenly concerned for my niece.

"She's okay. Well, she's in hospital, but she will be okay. However, she's in shock and hasn't said a word since a member of my team found her this morning."

Tears spilled from my eyes. "Oh, thank God. Please let her know I'm on my way."

I hung up and sat staring at the phone for the longest time.

I couldn't remember the last time I saw Steph. Each of us wrapped up in our own lives, we fell out of touch and had barely even spoke on the phone since our parents' accident, three years ago.

I tried to remember how old Diane would be—she must be a teenager now. Maybe older. Shit! How had I let it go so long? And now, with Steph gone, I would never get to see my baby sister again.

I was no stranger to the finality of death. First with my parents, and then Giles. Most people would think I'd want to be around family, not holed up in the villa alone.

I closed my eyes, trying to block the thoughts of my beautiful, vivacious sister. *Boop boop be doop.* I blinked back a fresh bout of tears at the memories of our teenage joke brought about because of Steph's voluptuous curves and jet-black curls. They were a far cry from my own pretzel-like limbs and frizzy blonde hair that I straightened when I stayed in the city.

CHAPTER 4

I sat staring into space, sobbing my heart out for the next three hours. I couldn't face getting dressed, and the thought of driving for a couple of hours made me want to curl up in bed and pull the duvet over my head.

I finally packed a bag and prepared to leave.

Half an hour later I took the lift to the parking level and loaded my bag into Giles' silver Land Rover Discovery. I could very easily take my own soft-top BMW, but I didn't know what my trip would entail. I might need a substantial car to collect Diane and her belongings.

It seemed strange to be driving on the left again. After three months in Spain, I'd completely adapted to driving on the right and knew I would need to be extra alert until I got used to being home.

I found the trip out of the city relatively smooth sailing. I was on the M61 heading towards Cumbria in record time and predicted I'd arrive in Carlisle by about 4pm.

Having eaten nothing since yesterday, I was feeling a little light-headed, but the thought of food made me nauseous.

I drove on autopilot, going over and over what the Detective had said. I hadn't been brave enough to check out what the news was saying about the double murder in such a small Cumbrian village, but I knew I would learn all the gory details soon enough.

The scenery changed, and miles and miles of rolling hills stretched out in front of me, but I couldn't enjoy it—not today. Would they need me to identify my sister's body? Terror gripped me and wouldn't let go.

Taking the exit for the sleepy village of Elsden, I suddenly remembered I needed to call the Detective back. Pulling over to the side of the winding country road, I hit redial.

"Conrad Jenkins," the same growly voice said.

"Hi Detective. It's Susanna Carmichael."

He paused just long enough to gather his thoughts. "Yes, hello, Ms Carmichael."

"You told me to let you know when I arrive. Well, I'm here."

"I must apologise, but something's come up that I can't get out of. Can we arrange to meet at six o'clock at the station?"

"Erm. Okay, I guess. I'll go over to the hospital to see Diane. Has there been any change there?"

"Not that I know of."

"Okay. Thank you. I'll see you later."

I was almost in Elsden, the village Steph and Eddie had lived in since they married around eighteen years ago. The quickest route would be to drive past their house and back onto the road to Carlisle.

I slowed the Land Rover as I approached the front of their house. My heartbeat thudded in my temples and I thought I might throw up.

A uniformed cop stood beside blue police tape that had been stretched across the driveway, and several people wearing white coveralls were standing beside the front entrance.

A sudden tightness in my chest forced me to pull over to the side of the road.

Was my sister still inside?

A painful emptiness twisted in my gut. Why had I left it so long? I hadn't even told her about Giles—preferring instead to deal with my grief alone. But now I needed her. I needed one of her all-encompassing hugs. I needed to hear her hearty, infectious laugh. I just needed my sister. Burying my head in my hands, deep sobs wracked my body.

A while later, I wiped my eyes and glanced at the clock. Almost 5pm. I needed to get my skates on if I was to call in to see Diane before my meeting with the Detective.

It took twenty minutes to cross to the hospital on the other side of Carlisle.

I climbed from the Land Rover and gasped. It was bloody cold. So used to the Spanish climate, I'd forgotten to pack a cardigan, or a jacket. I was such a twit.

I approached the main desk in the hospital. "Could you tell me where I can find Diane Hewitt, please?"

The friendly faced woman nodded and tapped her keyboard several times. "Yes. She's on the first floor—1C. Ask a member of staff on the desk there, and they'll help you."

I glanced at my watch. 5.30pm. It didn't give me long to spend with my niece before I would have to leave to meet up with the Detective. I followed the signs to 1C and asked an effeminate male nurse at the desk where I could find her.

"Are you a relative?"

"Yes. I'm her aunt."

"You do know what's happened, don't you?"

I nodded. "Of course, I do," I said impatiently. "My sister and her husband have been murdered."

"I'm sorry. This way, please."

He led me down a corridor to a room on the left. "Your niece is in here. She hasn't spoken or acknowledged anybody since she arrived."

"Is that normal?" I asked.

"The brain is a complex instrument. In times of immense

trauma, it can sometimes shut off in order to block out terrifying memories."

"How long will it last?"

"There's no telling. We just have to be patient. I'm sorry I can't be more helpful."

"No, that's fine. Thanks."

I watched as he walked away. Then, bracing myself, I entered the room.

The last time I'd seen Diane she was a cute little dark-haired kid. I remembered she liked to play the violin, badly in my opinion, and loved to be the centre of attention. I knew she would've changed, but I wasn't expecting a bleached-blonde teenager with black roots and gaunt, sunken eyes.

I stepped backwards convinced the silly man had taken me to the wrong room, but then I saw the name above the bed. Diane Hewitt. I spun away from her and out into the corridor. How the hell had Steph allowed her pretty little daughter to do that to herself? And what kind of sister was I to stay away from my only family for all this time?

I couldn't face going back inside. Not yet, anyway.

It suddenly occurred to me I had nowhere to stay tonight. I decided to ask the Detective to recommend somewhere.

"Everything okay?" the man on the desk asked as he saw me striding from the ward.

"I just received a call from the police—they want to see me. What time does visiting end?"

"Ah, don't worry about that—she's in a private ward. Just come back when you can."

"Okay, thanks," I glanced at his name badge, "Jason."

Back at the car, I searched the sat-nav for the local police station. There were two addresses which confused me, so I googled the main one and set the destination.

The building was huge. I parked the car and called the Detective's number.

"Conrad Jenkins."

"Hi Detective. It's Susanna Carmichael."

"I'm not far away, Ms Carmichael. I got waylaid."

"I'm just outside the station. Wasn't sure where to go."

"Yeah, it can be a little confusing. We can meet in town if you like?"

"Actually, I was going to ask if you could recommend a hotel."

"You can't go wrong with The Thistle. Shall I meet you there? It's on the corner of the main roundabout at the top of town."

"Okay. See you there."

The Thistle Hotel was an impressive traditional, red stone building connected to a restaurant and bar. I rang the bell on the counter and the attractive, middle-aged barman rushed around to serve me. He had kind green eyes and wispy reddish hair that was thinning on top.

"Sorry, love. Short staffed today. Everyone's down with the dreaded lurgy."

"The lurgy?"

"Flu. Half the town's down with it. What can I do for you?"

"Do you have any vacancies?"

He scanned the computer screen. "You're in luck. It's a double, mind. Is that okay?"

"Perfect."

"If you'll just fill out this form."

Once we'd finalised the paperwork, he handed me a key card.

"Your room is on the second floor, number 206. I would offer to carry your case, but..." He nodded towards the bar.

"That's fine. Thanks a lot."

I trudged up two grand, sweeping flights of stairs and found 206 at the end of the corridor.

The room was large and airy, with a country cottage feel to it. A king-sized bed lined one wall, with an old-fashioned fireplace opposite. A comfy looking armchair sat beside the bay window overlooking the immaculately kept rear gardens. I could even see the famous Carlisle Castle from where I stood.

Opening up my case, I took out another long-sleeved T-shirt and slipped it on over the top of the one I was wearing. It would have to do until tomorrow when I'd need to go clothes shopping.

I made my way back down to the bar, unsure of what the Detective would want of me.

"What can I get you, Miss? The first drink's on the house," the barman said.

"I'll have a glass of your house red, please."

"Coming right up." He grinned. "So, what brings you to this neck of the woods?"

"Family."

"Have you been on holiday? You don't get a tan like that from our disappointing British summertime."

"Spain. Just got back yesterday."

"Lucky thing. What I wouldn't give for a week in the sun."

"You'd have to pay staff if you went on holiday," a familiar gruff voice said. "And we all know what a skinflint you are."

"Hello, Jenkins, me old mate. To what do we owe the pleasure?" the barman said.

I quickly turned to put a face to the name and was surprised to see Detective Jenkins was nothing like I'd imagined. He was tall, well over six feet, and broad. His hair was luscious—thick waves of black deliciousness, and he had a full, highly-groomed beard. But it was the piercing blue eyes that caught my attention and caused my pulse to quicken.

CHAPTER 5

"Hi, Detective," I said, flustered.

"Ms Carmichael. Sorry I'm late."

"Susanna, please."

"Shall we?" He indicated one of the booths.

I picked up my glass and slid down from the stool.

He stepped to the side and motioned for me to go ahead of him. "A pint of bitter, if you don't mind, Ryan," he called over his shoulder.

"I'll fetch it over."

"Good man."

I scooted into the booth and sipped at the wine.

The Detective sat opposite me with those distracting blue eyes of his. "I'm sorry about your sister."

"Thanks. To be honest I'm still in shock."

"Unfortunately so are we. We're hoping when your niece wakes up she'll be able to shed some light on what happened. At the moment we're treating it as a foiled robbery."

The barman approached and placed a pint of dark brown liquid in front of the Detective.

I waited until he left before continuing. "I don't get it. Why would a thief kill them?"

"Maybe they knew him."

"Him? So you know it was a man?"

"Just going off what Diane said during the 999 call. She said *he* had killed her dad and probably her mum too."

"How did they die?"

He slowly rubbed his temple. "It appears they'd both received fatal stab wounds—although we're still awaiting the post-mortem results."

I buried my head in my hands. A huge knot of grief gripped the centre of my chest as I thought of my beautiful sister's body slashed and torn. "I can't believe it. Poor Steph." I sniffed and wiped my nose on my sleeve. "Sorry," I said, catching his disgusted expression.

"It's fine." He handed me a tissue.

I took it. "Thanks," I said, wiping my face.

"Did you manage to see Diane?" he asked.

"I didn't get there until late and she was out of it. A member of staff said I could go back later."

He nodded. "Can you tell me about your relationship with your sister?"

"So-so. To be honest, I haven't seen her in a few years."

"Why's that?"

I blew my nose and took a trembling breath. "Oh, you know—life. I was busy." I laughed sadly. "Too busy for my own sister."

"Hey, don't blame yourself. It's more common than you think."

"Yeah?"

He nodded. "I'm afraid so."

"Thanks. The truth is I've been too busy. Steph and Eddie were the opposite of Giles and me. They were steady, dependable. We even called them boring." My breath hitched.

"And you?"

"We were the original jet setters. Giles owned a number of

international businesses and we were regularly flitting between Manchester and New York."

"Nice."

"At first, maybe."

"Owned?"

"Sorry?"

"You said he *owned* a number of businesses."

"Giles died. A little over three months ago. The ninth of May to be exact."

"I'm sorry. That's rough."

"That's why I went to Spain. I couldn't face being at home—home makes it real somehow."

"I understand. What brought you back?"

"I needed to sort some things out. Check on the apartment, decide where I want to be—that sort of thing."

"I see."

"So, will I need to identify them?"

"It's not necessary. Edward's brother has done it already."

I blew out in short bursts in an effort to control my raging heartbeat.

He took a deep swig of his pint and I had to force my hands to stay on the table and not wipe away the frothy white foam from his moustache.

He must've read my mind, as he licked it off before smoothing his moustache down with his fingers. "I don't normally drink when on duty, but I'll be going home after here."

"That's fine. Is there anything else I can do?"

"Not really."

"Will I have to take Diane in? Or have Edward's family stepped up?"

"I don't know, I'm sorry. Maybe you can discuss Diane's future with them once she's ready to leave hospital."

"And my sister and Eddie? When will their bodies be released?"

"Again, I'm sorry, I don't know. I'll keep you updated."

"So, you have no suspects?"

"Nothing yet. The SOCO team is still going through the property, and we have another team of officers making house-to-house calls. We're hoping somebody might have seen something."

"Was there a lot of blood?"

He was looking uncomfortable.

"If there was a lot of blood, the killer must've been covered in it too, which means there's more chance of witnesses, surely?"

"Yes, exactly. Believe me, Susanna, we're taking this case very seriously."

"I didn't mean to imply you're not doing your job, Detective. I'm just trying to understand the situation, that's all."

"It's Conrad, seeing as we're on first name terms." He drained the rest of his glass and shuffled his bulky body from the booth.

CHAPTER 6

Once the Detective had left, I decided to try to eat something before heading back to the hospital. The wine, although welcome, had caused my legs to feel like jelly.

"Can I see a menu, please?" I asked the barman.

"We only have bar snacks in here. Otherwise we do a full menu next door in the restaurant."

"A bar snack is fine." I smiled, conscious of how shitty I must look after crying my heart out.

He handed me a black laminated menu. "You okay, love?"

I felt a lump form in my throat rendering me speechless. I nodded pressing a finger to my lips and blinking back the tears.

"Take a seat, and I'll come for your order in a few minutes. Would you like a top up?" he lifted a bottle of wine.

"No, I'd best not. I need to drive later."

"Fair enough."

Three couples entered the bar, and I scurried off to my booth.

Ryan sauntered over a few minutes later with a pad and pen. "What do you fancy?"

"I'll just have the fish and chips, please."

"Mushy peas?"

"Of course." I tried to grin.

My eyes felt heavy and scratchy. I'd spent the first two-and-a-half months crying after Giles died, and, although the tears had steadied off the past few weeks, I thought I'd be used to crying by now, but I wasn't.

I picked at the food. Although my stomach was growling, it refused to accept any sustenance.

"Something wrong?" Ryan asked as I placed the barely touched plate on the bar.

"No, the food is fine. It's just me."

"You sure?"

"Yes. Thank you."

I ran up to my room, washed my face and combed my hair. I was right, I looked terrible.

"Your sister just died." I justified my appearance to my reflection.

Fifteen minutes later, I entered the hospital and headed to the first floor.

"Good evening," a woman on the front desk said, raising her eyebrows in question.

"I'm here to see my niece, Diane Hewitt. Jason said it would be okay."

"No problem. Do you know where she is?"

I nodded and walked towards Diane's room.

The light was dim inside the room, and I held my breath as I entered.

A man dressed in jeans and a blue and white checked shirt was seated beside the bed. He jumped to his feet, startled, when he saw me.

"Oh, I'm sorry. I didn't know she had visitors."

The man, who appeared to be in his early forties, eyed me suspiciously. "Can I help you?"

"I'm Susanna. Diane's aunt."

His eyes widened. Giving me a closed lip smile, he nodded.

I wondered what he thought he knew about me. He'd clearly heard something. "And you are?"

"Robert Hewitt. Eddie's brother."

"Have we met?" I tried to place him from Steph and Eddie's wedding.

He shrugged gruffly. "Dunno."

I felt self-conscious. "How is she?" I nodded at Diane.

"No change." He sat back down—no offer of a seat for me.

What a gent. "Awful isn't it? I still can't believe it."

He stared at Diane's face without responding.

Suddenly feeling like an intruder, I walked alongside the bed, stroking the girl's hand. "What did the doctor say?"

"She's in shock. Her brain's gone into self-preservation mode —whatever that's supposed to fucking mean."

His sudden anger shocked me. "God only knows what the poor girl witnessed."

Robert suddenly spun away, sending the chair clattering to the floor. He strode over to the window. His shoulders were taut as he placed both hands on the windowsill and bent forwards staring out at the night.

The sudden movement caused my already racing heartbeat to go into overdrive. I steadied myself on the bed, trembling uncontrollably.

A few minutes later, Robert dropped his hands to his side, turned to face the room, and leaned his bottom on the windowsill. "I'm sorry."

I nodded, too scared to speak.

"I'm just so fucking angry. I mean, who would do this?"

Tears welled and spilled from my eyes at the rawness of his words.

"What did my brother—your sister, ever do to anyone? They were the most decent people I'd ever met." His own tears began to flow, which shocked me even more than the earlier outburst.

I walked around the bed following instinct rather than common sense, and I pulled him into my arms.

He buried his head in my hair and sobbed—deep, gut-wrenching sobs.

"I know. I know," I said, stroking his hair.

"Uncle Rob?" a little voice said, startling us both apart.

"Princess," he said, racing to the bedside. "Thank God. Oh, thank God." He kissed her head repeatedly.

He settled back down beside her, holding her hand to his lips.

She glanced at me questioningly.

"Hi, Diane. I'm your—"

"I know who you are," she whispered, glaring at me.

Surprised by her hostility, I tentatively approached the other side of the bed.

She ignored me and turned back to Robert. "Mum and Dad, are they…?"

He nodded, a pained expression etched on his face.

She lay back into her pillow and stared at the ceiling. Her chin trembled, and her breathing became laboured.

Robert stroked her hair whispering words of love and support in her ear. "Do you remember what happened?" he asked a few minutes later.

She gave two slow nods of her head.

Robert quickly glanced at me, gulped, then chewed at his lips for a second. "Can you tell me what you remember?"

She closed her eyes as though trying to block it out.

"Maybe we should wait until the police are here to save her having to dredge it all up twice."

Robert nodded.

"I'll call them." I stepped into the corridor and hit redial.

"Conrad Jenkins."

"Hi, it's Susanna. Diane's awake, and she said she remembers what happened. I wondered if—"

"I'm on my way."

CHAPTER 7

Less than fifteen minutes later, DI Jenkins tapped on the window and beckoned for us to step outside.

"So, what did she tell you?" he said.

I shook my head. "Nothing yet. We wanted to wait for you. It's going to be bad enough recalling it all once, never mind twice."

He nodded. "Good call. Thanks for that. Shall we?" He indicated the door.

Robert and I returned to our earlier positions, and the Detective stood at the end of the bed.

"Hey, Diane," he said, as softly as his gravelly voice would allow.

"Hi."

The detective looked at me, clearly uncomfortable.

I smiled my encouragement.

She tilted her head back in acknowledgement.

"Your aunt tells me you remember what happened?"

Robert leaned forward, grabbing Diane's hand.

She stiffened. "I know he killed them." Her eyes suddenly filled with tears.

"Who?" The detective said. "Did you see him?"

"No. But I heard him."

"Can you go through it for me? I know it's painful, but we really need you to tell us every detail however small. Do you think you can manage that?"

She glanced at me and then at Robert before nodding again.

The detective took out his phone and pressed a few buttons. "If you don't mind, I'll record you. This will prevent us having to go over and over it. Okay?"

"Yes."

"Right, in your own time, and from the very beginning, can you tell me what happened?"

"I got home late. I'd been at my boyfriend's, and Dad went berserk when I came home."

"What time? Do you remember?"

"Around 2am. I thought they would be in bed, and I snuck in planning on creeping to my room to avoid a fight. We'd done nothing but fight for weeks." She closed her eyes wrapping her arms around herself.

"It's okay, Princess. Just take your time," Robert said.

"I found Dad sitting in the dark. I'd never seen him so angry before. He yelled at me. I ended up running to my room and slamming the door. I cried myself to sleep."

"Then what happened?" I asked. Although desperate to know, I dreaded hearing the details of what had actually happened to my sister.

"My dad started shouting again. I was scared he was going to come upstairs and bawl at me again. I pulled the duvet over my head and prayed to God he wouldn't."

"He was still downstairs at that stage?" the Detective asked.

She nodded. "I think so. That's what it sounded like anyway. Then I heard a loud bang. I now know the vase of dried flowers had fallen off the hall table on the turnaround landing of the stairs, but I didn't know what made the sound at the time." Tears ran down her face and off the end of her chin, soaking the neck of the light blue hospital gown she wore. "It was Mum's screams that made me get out of bed. At first I thought Dad was hurting her."

"Had he hurt her before?" Jenkins asked.

"I beg your pardon!" Robert's nostrils flared, and his eyes shot daggers at the Detective. "My brother worshipped his family. He wouldn't harm a hair on Steph's head."

"Mr Hewitt, I must ask you to be quiet and allow Diane to answer my questions."

Robert scowled and turned back to Diane. "Go on, Princess."

"No. Never. He was a softy usually. But that night he was angry. Really angry. Mum always took a sleeping pill, so I wasn't surprised she didn't wake up when he shouted at me. But when I heard her crying, I knew something was really wrong."

"So you got out of bed?"

She nodded, reaching for Robert's hand again. "I crept from my room," she whispered. "I can still hear her screams—it was awful."

"Here. Have a sip of water." Robert jumped to his feet and snatched up a glass from the table.

Diane sat upright, accepted the glass, and rubbed a shaking hand along her forehead before drinking deeply. After a brief pause, she handed the glass back to Robert and settled back against her pillows.

Hot bile raced up my throat. I rushed into the adjoining bathroom and threw up the meagre contents of my stomach. Then, after splashing my face with water, I walked back into the room, suddenly embarrassed that they would have heard everything. "I'm sorry," I said, trying to smile.

The Detective nodded and waited for me to return to my position at the side of the bed. "Shall I go and find another chair?"

"No. I'll be alright."

"Here, have this one," Robert said, suddenly shamefaced for not volunteering the chair earlier.

After a few moments, we all settled down again, me on the chair and Robert perched beside Diane on the edge of the bed.

"Okay, where were we?" Jenkins said.

All eyes back on Diane, she nodded. "I got out of bed and crept to my parents' bedroom. Mum's bedside lamp was on, and I saw her on her knees beside the bed. She was terrified." Diane's voice cracked, and she angrily wiped the tears from her face before continuing. "She saw me and shook her head. I knew she wanted me to get out of there, so I did."

Robert pulled her into his arms as she sobbed. "It's okay, I've got you."

"Did you see anybody else in the room?" I asked?

"The back of the man, that's all. I saw his reflection in the mirror, but I didn't see his face."

"What do you remember about him?" Jenkins altered his position and placed the phone on the end of the bed.

"He wasn't very big. Not as big as my dad. It looked like he had a grey T-shirt on."

"Anything else?"

She shook her head. "I don't think so. Although I feel there is more—I just can't put my finger on it."

"That's okay. You're doing really well," Robert said, stroking her straw-like hair.

"I ran for the stairs, and I noticed the vase was on the floor. I stepped over it, and that's when I saw him."

"Who?" Robert said.

"Dad." She buried her head in his shoulder.

"Maybe we should leave it there." Robert turned to the Detective. "She's too upset."

"No!" Diane said. "I need to do this, and then I don't want to think about it ever again." She cleared her throat and wiped her eyes in an attempt to compose herself. "Dad lay on the half-landing. Dead. His eyes were open, and he was covered in blood. I screamed. I couldn't help myself." She sobbed, looking at each of us in turn.

"It's okay." Robert rubbed her back.

"I could still hear Mum's cries at that point, then silence. I knew she was dead too."

Her words tore at my heart, but I had to be strong for Diane—it was clearly more upsetting for her having to relive it.

"I tried the front door, but it wouldn't budge. Then I heard the man moving about upstairs, so I ran into Dad's office. That's when I called the police. I really thought he was going to get me next. He kicked the office door in and I heard him breathing heavily right in front of me, and then the sound of sirens and flashing blue and red lights filled the room. I don't remember what happened after that."

CHAPTER 8

I walked the Detective out to the front desk.

"What now, Detective?"

"Please, call me Conrad."

"Sorry. Conrad."

"We were hoping Diane would have more details for us. I'm not going to lie to you, Susanna. We haven't found much of anything at the crime scene. No DNA, no bloody footprints, no signs of a break in. Nothing."

I gasped. "You're joking?"

He shook his head. "I'm sorry. But like I said earlier, it's still early days, so all is not lost. But the more time passes the less likely we are to find anything useful."

"So he could get away with it?"

"I sincerely hope not. And I give you my word I'll do all I can to catch the bastard who did this."

"I hope so. I can't bear the thought of that man walking the street, breathing in air even, after taking my sister's life."

"Do you mind if I ask a personal question?"

"Go on."

"Didn't you like your brother-in-law?"

I rubbed my forehead and then ran my fingers through my hair. "He was okay, I guess. But no, I didn't think very much of him."

"Why not? Most people who knew him can't speak more highly of him. You're the first person who's even suggested he might not be the most perfect human being."

"I didn't like the way he controlled Steph. She changed after she met him. Her views became his views. Her likes and loves and hobbies changed into his likes and loves and hobbies—as though he'd brainwashed her somehow. She looked like my sister, laughed like my sister, but it was superficial. She couldn't see it, of course. She was infatuated with him, and the hold he had over her reminded me of one of those weird cults you hear about. So, except for the occasional family get together, I decided to stay away."

"When did you last speak to her?"

"In person, probably a couple of years ago."

"In person?"

"Yeah, I mean I tried to call her before I went to Spain. Giles had just died, and I'd had quite a lot of wine. I needed her, but she wasn't home. I left a message with Eddie telling him I was going to be in Spain for a while and that I had my mobile with me if she wanted to return my call. But she didn't."

"Do you think he told her about your call?"

"No. I don't. For all that people say what a nice man he was, if you went against him in any way you'd know about it. He knew I didn't like him, and he didn't like me right back."

"Thanks for your honesty, Susanna. I'll let you get back to your niece."

I waited at the door as he walked away, and then I headed back inside.

Diane stopped sobbing as I entered.

"I'm sorry. Would you like me to go?"

"I don't know why you're here in the first place," she said spitefully, her lips in a fine line.

"She was my sister," I cried. "You're all I have left."

"Where've you been all these years? Off with that snooty husband of yours. You never cared about Mum when she was alive. Why should that change now?"

"Of course, I cared about her." I glanced at Robert for support, but he looked down at his hands.

"I loved her, Diane. She was my baby sister." Hot tears slid down my face.

The anger in Diane's eyes faded a little. It wasn't personal. She just needed to lash out at someone. I'd done the same after Giles died—I'd hated the world. But it didn't make her hostility towards me any easier. I don't know what I'd expected from this frantic girl, but I hadn't expected her to shun me.

"So where is your sugar daddy?" She looked me up and down as though I was a piece of particularly stinky shit.

"If you mean Giles, he's dead."

She gasped, and, right or wrong, I felt a wave of pleasure that my awful news had hit the mark.

"Mum didn't say."

"Because your mum didn't know. I rang to tell her before I went to Spain, but she never called me back."

"She did. She rang loads of times. She was going out of her mind trying to get hold of you."

I gasped. "Well, I never had any missed calls. Maybe your dad wrote down the wrong number?" A fresh bout of tears filled my eyes. Steph hadn't forgotten about me after all. I dragged a scrunched-up tissue from my pocket and dabbed at the corners of my eyes.

"How did he die?"

The dreaded question. My head spun, and I fought to swallow a lump in my throat. "I-I can't…" I closed my eyes. "It's too raw."

"I'm sorry."

"You weren't to know, sweetheart. And I will tell you, but today's been too emotional as it is."

"Right." Robert got to his feet. "Maybe you should try to get some shut-eye. I'll come back in the morning."

"Yes. He's right. I just want to add I'm here for you, Diane. Whatever happens, you're my only living relative, and I want to play a more active role."

"I'd like that."

Robert and I kissed her goodnight, and she snuggled back down in the bed. Then we accompanied each other to the car park.

"She's changed so much," I said, once we were out of earshot. "What happened to those lovely black curls?"

Robert smiled sadly. "She's been a bit of a handful of late. Steph and Eddie have been beside themselves."

"What happened?"

"Who knows? Mixing with the wrong crowd—rebelling against Eddie's controlling nature. I've been hoping it's just a phase. She's a good kid at heart."

"I know. I can tell. Any idea of what she'll do now? I don't mind taking her in, but I'm aware your side of the family may prefer her to stay in the area."

"My parents are in no position to take on a young girl. They moved back to Ireland, and they've not been well. My job has me all over the country, so, although I'd love her to come to stay with me, it wouldn't work, I'm afraid."

I wanted to ask if he was married or had a family of his own, but I guessed I'd find out soon enough.

CHAPTER 9

I tossed and turned in the comfortable hotel bed, but, although exhausted, sleep once again eluded me.

My eyes seemed compelled to watch each luminous green number of the clock roll around until outside the birds began their day. The curtains didn't keep out a bit of light so I gave up trying to sleep.

Stumbling to the bathroom, I filled the old-fashioned clawfoot bath with steaming bubbles then I eased my aching bones into them.

The next thing I knew, the water was stone-cold. Now I knew the trick of grabbing a few hours of sleep. I just wished I'd worked it out earlier.

I clambered from the bath, shivering, and jumped into the shower to thaw myself out. How had I managed to sleep so soundly immersed in cold water when I hadn't managed a wink in the most comfy bed ever?

"Good morning, Miss Carmichael," Ryan said as I walked down the stairs. "Are you joining us for breakfast?"

My stomach growled—it had been days since I'd eaten a proper meal. "Yes, I think I will. And, please, call me Susanna."

He walked me through to the deserted restaurant.

"Still a one-man band, is it?"

"I have a chef, thank goodness. But the rest is down to me."

"You must be run ragged," I said, taking a seat at the table nearest the door.

"You could say that." He handed me a menu.

"I'll just have tea and toast if that's okay?"

"Be right back."

I checked my phone and remembered what Diane told me about Steph trying to call. I wasn't sure if it made me happier that she hadn't actually ignored me or sad because I missed out on the last conversation I could've had with my sister.

"Good old tea and toast," Ryan said, placing the tray on an empty table and bringing over the items one by one.

"Thanks for that."

"So, how do you know Conrad?"

"I don't really. It was business."

"Not the murder?"

"What makes you think that?"

"It's all anybody's talking about. Murder is a big deal in these parts. So, is it?"

I sighed. "Yes. Steph was my sister."

"I'm so sorry. That's awful. Conrad will catch him. He's a top Detective."

Twenty minutes later, I left the hotel and headed for the hospital. It was still raining—the sky thick with miserable grey clouds, which was a far cry from the vivid blueness of the Spanish sky I'd been used to.

"Hi," Diane said shyly, from her hospital bed.

"Hey, how are you feeling?"

"Better. The doctor said I can go home today."

"That's good—isn't it?"

"I don't have a home."

"You can come to the hotel with me if you like?"

"I told Uncle Rob I'd go to his house, but…" She looked up at me, hopefully. "I was going to ask if you'd come too."

"Me?" I was staggered. I couldn't get over the change of heart. I'd been the big bad wolf just last night.

She nodded. "He has enough room, and it'll be nice to be able to spend time together."

"Well, I guess I could. I've already booked the hotel for the rest of the week, but I'll see if I can get out of it." As I said the words, my pulse quickened. I didn't know Robert and didn't particularly like him. I found him a bit creepy if I was totally honest, which wasn't surprising seeing he was Eddie's brother. However, I couldn't say that to Diane who seemed to adore her uncle.

"I might have a shower. That nice Detective is going to bring me some of my clothes soon. He said our house is still classed as a crime scene, so we're not allowed to go ourselves."

I helped her out of bed and into the bathroom. Her build was nothing like her mother's. In fact, I couldn't see any resemblance at all. She looked more like her father. I hoped she hadn't got his personality.

Conrad arrived as I waited for Diane. I was flicking through a magazine.

"I've got some of Diane's things," he said, placing a small pink overnight bag on the bed.

"Any updates?" I asked.

"Nothing yet. All the neighbours have been questioned, and nobody saw or heard a thing. How is Diane today?"

"She seems much brighter."

"Good. I want to ask a few more questions. I didn't want to overload her last night."

"She's in the shower. She shouldn't be too long."

The door to the bathroom opened, and Diane peered out. "Oh, hi. Can you pass me my clothes, please?"

Conrad handed her the bag, and she closed the door again.

"She's going to stay at Robert's, and she's asked me to go too," I said.

"And will you?"

"I think I should. Diane and I need to establish a relationship. From what Robert said, she can't stay with him indefinitely as he works away a lot."

"Will you take her to Manchester?"

"Who's going to Manchester?" Diane said as she came from the bathroom dressed in ripped light blue jeans and black, tight-fitting T-shirt. "Are you talking about me?"

I glanced at Conrad before speaking. "It's early days, Diane. We're just tossing around a few ideas."

"But I can't go to Manchester. All my friends are here."

"We don't have to worry about any of that yet, love. Don't work yourself up."

"You must be pleased the doctors said you can leave?" Conrad said.

"I dunno. I can't go home."

"No, not yet." He seemed uncomfortable. "I have a couple of questions for you, and then I'll get on my way."

"More questions?"

"Just a couple."

"Go on, then." She perched on the edge of the bed.

"Can you tell me your boyfriend's name and address, please?"

"What do you want that for? Do you think he did it?"

Conrad shook his head. "No, not at all. It's just to tidy up the loose ends."

"Don't hassle him. He doesn't like the pigs—I mean cops."

"What's his name?"

"Andre Cooper. He lives—"

"I know where he lives."

"What's that supposed to mean?"

"What?"

"I know where he lives," she mimicked.

Conrad raised his eyebrows. "What do you think it means?"

"I think you're being smart. Just because you know of him, you're thinking he could've broken into my home and butchered my family."

"You don't know what I'm thinking. Is this what you're thinking?"

"Go fuck yourself."

"Diane!" I yelped, totally horrified.

"Well, I knew he'd do this. Can't find the real killer, so he'll try to pin it on an easy target. Andre wouldn't hurt a fly."

"Okay," Conrad shook his head. "Have you noticed anything strange over the past few weeks? You said your dad was acting strange on the night of his murder, but how about in the weeks leading up to that night?"

She closed her eyes and rubbed them. "I can't think of anything. Dad worked a lot and Mum was always doing housework or cleaning. She rarely went out, and I can't remember the last time she had any friends around."

"Did your dad have any close friends?"

"No. Not outside of work. That's why they didn't like me having a life. They expected me to want to spend all my time with them, like it used to be. The only person who would come around regularly was Uncle Rob."

"One last question. Is there anybody—either a neighbour, or your dad's work colleagues, who your dad had any problems with?"

"Not unless you count Dad's business partner. They had an

argument a few weeks ago. I don't know what it was about. Mum and Dad wouldn't discuss it in front of me, but they were both upset by it."

Conrad pulled at his bottom lip. "Okay. That's great. I'll be in touch." He smiled at us both before scooting out the door and down the corridor.

I was in no doubt Diane's boyfriend and Eddie's business partner would be dragged over the coals before sundown.

"Okay. If you're ready, I guess we should go. Is Robert expecting you?"

"He said he was busy, but that he'd leave the key for us to let ourselves in."

"And I'm guessing you know the way?"

She rolled her eyes. "Of course, I do. His house backs onto ours."

My breath hitched in my throat. "Do you think that's a good idea? Being so close to where it all happened?"

"What choice do I have? And plus all my friends live around there."

"Okay. Let's get going." I picked up her bag and linked my arm through hers.

CHAPTER 10

"Flash car," Diane said as I opened the back door of the Land Rover.

"It belonged to Giles. I just haven't had the heart to get rid of it."

"I wouldn't get rid of it—it's dope."

"Dope?"

She squinted at me. "Don't tell me you've never heard of dope?"

"Of course, I have. Someone who's a bit stupid is a dope and wacky baccy is sometimes called dope. Neither of these explanations could describe a car."

"It means awesome, great."

I threw her bag in the back and slammed the door. "I'll take your word for it."

"Do you need to pick anything up? A cardigan or a jacket?" I asked, looking at the goose pimples on her arms.

"I'm not allowed to go home for anything."

"No, I know that. I meant I'll buy you whatever you need. I need some extra clothes too because I forgot to pack enough."

She shrugged. "Okay, if you're sure."

"You'll need to tell me where to go, though."

"My favourite shop's on the high street."

"Perfect. Which way?"

We stopped off at the store and bought her a black jersey and a black puffa jacket. I chose a couple of cardigans, an orange fleece, and a red puffa jacket.

"Do you always wear bright colours?" she asked, eyeballing my cerise pink top.

"I do. Do you always wear black?"

"No. Not always. I sometimes wear grey." She grinned and, for the first time, I saw an inkling of the child I'd met years ago.

"You have lovely teeth," I said.

"That's random."

"Your mum always had perfect teeth. You get that from her."

"What's wrong with your teeth?"

"Nothing now. But I had to wear a brace for most of my teens. You don't know how lucky you are."

"Fuck that!"

"Hey! Language."

"Sorry."

"Did your parents allow you to swear like that?"

Her expression suddenly changed, and I felt bad for bringing it up. "My mum hated it. She was always telling me to stop."

"Then why didn't you? Our mum would've washed our mouths out with soap if we'd cursed like that. And I'm not talking the eff word, either."

"Yeah, but that was years ago. Everyone swears now."

"Not everyone. Respectful people don't swear."

"Do you swear?"

"I'm not saying I never swear, but when I do people sit up and take notice. If you're effing and jeffing every two minutes, it loses its power."

"I never thought of it like that."

I grinned. "Are you serious or are you taking the mick?"

"No. I'm serious. Put it this way, it's the best argument for not swearing I've ever heard. And believe me, Mum tried everything." She turned to look out of the window.

I glanced at her a couple of times sensing she had slumped into a place of grief. "Are you okay?"

She nodded still turned away.

"Tell me about your boyfriend."

"You won't like him. Adults never do."

"Why's that? Is he disrespectful?"

"No. He has a couple of piercings…" she paused, "…in his face."

I shrugged. "Does he treat you right?"

"Always."

"Then that's all I'm concerned about at this stage. But DI Jenkins seemed to know him. Is he a bad lad?"

"He's picked on a lot because of the way he looks. He's lovely when you get to know him."

"And I'm guessing your parents didn't like him?"

"They didn't like anyone—and I'm not exaggerating."

"I know your father could be a little controlling. I've seen it with my own eyes. But never doubt that they both loved you more than life itself."

"You're like her, you know?" Diane said.

"Who?"

"Mum. I didn't think you were anything alike, but I was wrong. You even sound like her sometimes."

"I hope you take comfort from that, because I can't shut up. It's not in my nature." I smiled hoping she would smile too.

She did.

"Okay. Which way?"

"Turn the next right, and Uncle Rob's house is along there on the left."

I followed her directions and pulled up in front of a surprisingly impressive red brick, semi-detached house.

The gardens were immaculately kept which surprised me. I

couldn't imagine Robert getting down and dirty amongst the flowerbeds. The property had square lines including the bay window—it was attractive but very masculine.

I grabbed Diane's bag from the car.

"Wait there a sec." Diane headed around the back of the house. She reappeared moments later holding the key. "Got it."

I followed her to the brightly painted, red front door. "Nice house."

"It's gorgeous. I love staying here." She unlocked the door and it swung open giving me the first view of the immaculate interior.

"I must admit, I didn't imagine his house would be like this. I thought it would be more along the lines of a bachelor pad."

"He's had this for a few years now. He bought it just before he married Kate."

"Oh, I didn't know he was married."

I stepped inside onto the herringbone wooden flooring taking in the light airiness of the hallway. A long hallstand held several silver photo frames, and the grey runner matched the carpet on the sweeping staircase.

"He's not anymore. Kate ran off with his best mate a couple of years ago. He lives alone."

"This is a beautiful home. It must take a lot of upkeep for one person."

The hall opened up to the spacious living room. A pale green, shaggy rug lay beside an ornate marble fireplace, and two large, pale gold chesterfield sofas had been placed to get the best view of the massive TV on the wall. The room was flooded with light from two picture windows and showcased ornate ceilings, wall panels and cornices.

"You're joking, aren't you? He has a housekeeper and a grounds man."

"What does he do for a job?"

"He's in IT. He works—he worked for Dad. Come on, I'll show you through the house."

The kitchen was stunning. High ceilings painted brilliant white. A farmhouse-style table sat in the bay window. There was a large central island, and an old-fashioned range cooker. There wasn't a thing out of place. I loved it.

"There's a downstairs bathroom through there." Diane pointed to a door beside the kitchen as we headed to the stairs.

Upstairs, the master bedroom would've fit my entire Spanish villa in it and still had room for the huge bed.

"It's like a show home. I'd be terrified of doing anything to make it look untidy."

"Nah, Uncle Rob doesn't care. He's not tidy. I swear." She walked into the room across the hall. "This is my bedroom."

Her room was smaller, and although still decorated in muted neutral tones, there was a little more colour in the bedding and curtains than I'd seen in the rest of the house so far.

"Nice," I said.

"And if you decide to…" she walked along the landing and threw open another door. "…this will be your room."

"I don't know, Diane. I'll probably just stay at the hotel for now."

Instant tears filled her eyes, and I realised she wasn't coping as well as I thought. "Don't cry. It will be fine." I wrapped my arms around her and she let loose, sobbing into my chest. I ended up shedding a few tears of my own.

Diane eventually stepped away from me and wiped her face with her hands. "Sorry."

"Hey, don't you apologise. It will hit you in waves. That's normal, and you mustn't try to supress it, okay?"

"I just want you here. I know it sounds silly, but it feels like a little bit of Mum is here."

That choked me and I struggled to swallow past a brick sized lump in my throat. "Okay. If Robert doesn't mind me being here, I'll stay."

"You will?" she squealed and launched herself into my arms again.

"Anybody home?" Robert called up the stairs.

"Hi, Uncle Rob." Diane walked towards the stairs holding my hand tightly. "We're up here."

Robert was hanging his jacket in the hall cupboard as we walked down the stairs.

"You have a beautiful home, Robert," I said. "Simply stunning."

"And Aunt Susie said she'll stay here with us, if you don't mind."

I was surprised by the easy way she said my name. I had been concerned over what she'd be comfortable calling me. I needn't have worried.

Robert shrugged. "Stay as long as you like."

Diane beamed, and I didn't want to make her cry again, so I nodded my thanks, but I felt a wave of hostility coming from Robert.

"Can I use your phone, Uncle Rob?"

"Yeah. Where's yours?"

"I think the police have it."

He handed her his mobile, unlocking the screen with his thumb print.

"Thanks. Can I give Talia and Andre this number?"

"Go for it. I'll take you into town and buy you a new one, if you like?" he offered.

"Would you?"

"Sure. Let me get changed, and I'll be right with you."

"I'll go and collect my things then if you don't mind, Diane?" I said.

"Okay. But don't be too long, will you?" Diane said, her eyebrows furrowed.

"I'll be there and back before you know it."

Diane took her bag upstairs.

"You'll need this." Robert handed me the spare key from the hall table. "In case you're back before us."

"Thanks. Are you sure you don't mind?" I said.

"I'm open to whatever Diane wants right now. She wants you here, so that's alright with me." He walked off without another word leaving me standing awkwardly in the hall.

Tosser.

CHAPTER 11

I found Ryan behind the bar again when I arrived at the hotel.

"Hey, Susanna. How's your day been?"

"Oh, you know. So, so, I guess. But I'm afraid I won't be needing the room anymore."

"Really? You heading back home already?"

"No. I'm going to stay with my niece—she needs me right now."

"Ah, understandable."

"I'll pay to the end of the week, of course."

"No way. I won't hear of it."

"Thank you, Ryan. You're a diamond. I'll just run up and get my stuff."

"No hurry. Would you like a drink?"

I hesitated, not really wanting to hang around, yet I felt it was the least I could do with him being so understanding. "Yes, that would be lovely. I'll have a shandy when I come back down. Won't be a tick.

It didn't take long to collect my things together as I hadn't yet unpacked.

"That was quick," Ryan said as I returned. He nodded to the glass of shandy on the bar.

"Thanks. Aren't you joining me?"

"Oh, go on then. Why not?" He poured himself a pint of something dark with a creamy white head—it reminded me of Guinness only not as black. Then he picked up the glass and carried it around to my side of the bar and climbed up onto a stool beside me.

"So," I said, suddenly lost for words. It was one thing chatting to a man behind the bar, but it was another thing entirely sitting side by side. More intimate somehow.

"Do you live full time in Spain?" He sipped his beer.

"I don't know." Then I laughed, realising how stupid that sounded. "I mean, I hadn't planned it, but I've been there for three months and didn't want to return."

"Return to where? Where's home?"

"Manchester. Or should I say it used to be? Now I don't know where I actually think of as home. Maybe it is Spain."

"Do you still have property in Manchester?"

"Yes. An apartment, and I love it, but it holds too many bad memories."

"I know what you mean. Since my wife walked out on me, I've often wondered what the hell I'm doing here—running myself ragged and for what?"

I sipped at my drink and nodded, raising my eyebrows in agreement. "Hard, isn't it?"

"Are you married?"

I nodded then changed the nod to a shake as I fingered my wedding ring. "No, I mean. My husband died."

"That stinks."

"Anyway, I'd best be off. I told Diane I wouldn't be long. Can I settle my bill?"

"How about you pop by later on in the week? I'll have to prepare your invoice and the printer is up in my suite."

"Are you sure? I'm happy to just pay. I don't need an invoice."

"I like to keep it above board. I don't need the tax man on my tail."

"I guess not. Okay, see you soon and thanks for your hospitality."

He jumped from the stool and collected the glasses then bent in to kiss my cheek.

Startled, I jumped backwards and then laughed feeling jittery all of a sudden. "I'm sorry. Guess I'm more highly strung than I thought."

"Don't worry about it." He grinned and headed behind the bar.

When I got back to Robert's, the house was empty. I contemplated sitting in the car, a little uncomfortable about letting myself in, but I was aware how stupid that would look to an already disapproving Robert. Leaving my case in the car, I entered and sat on one of the pristine sofas waiting for them to return.

Half an hour later, I heard the garage door judder open, and I sat up straight unsure what to do with myself. I hated feeling like this. The last time I'd stayed at someone's house was before my parents died three years ago.

"Hi, Aunt Susie," Diane said, suddenly appearing in the hallway.

I hadn't realised the garage had an internal door, and I jumped out of my skin. "Oh, hi." I studied her face and could tell she'd been crying. "Are you okay?"

"No. I'm pissed off."

"Just in general, or has something else happened?"

"The Detective has only gone and arrested Andre. His mum said they woke him up and had a warrant to search the house and everything! His uncle's with him."

"Hey," Robert appeared behind her and placed several shopping bags on the coffee table.

"I guess they have to question everybody. If he's innocent, he'll be released. You'll see."

"That's what I told her," Robert said.

"Yeah, but you also said a lot of other stuff. And it's not fair."

"Tough. I meant it. If they find out that nasty piece of work has touched my brother, I'll kill him with my bare hands."

My breath hitched in my throat. I hated any form of conflict nowadays.

I reached for Diane's hand and pulled her down onto the sofa beside me. "Ignore him," I whispered when Robert left the room. "He's just upset, that's all. Men have a different way of coping than us."

"He's also been to see Dad's solicitor about the will."

My skin tingled. "Really? Already?"

"I'm one of the executors," Robert said, startling me again with his sudden appearance. He wasn't normal. What type of man makes no sound on a wooden floor?

"Oh, okay."

"Yes. We need to discuss some things. The solicitor is dealing with most of it, but I told him I'd catch you up initially."

I wasn't ready for this. Steph and Eddie weren't even cold yet, and this guy was ready to pick through their belongings. "Can't it wait? We need to get through the funeral arrangements first."

"That's as may be, but there are a number of things we need to discuss as soon as possible."

"Like what?"

"Maybe I should give you a copy of the document, and then we can discuss anything of relevance?"

"I want to know too." Diane jumped to her feet and began pacing the rug. "You can't leave me out."

I glanced at Robert and raised my eyebrows, unsure if she should see it or not. He knew the contents, not me.

"We can discuss the main points after dinner, if you like? All together."

I nodded and looked at Diane, who also seemed happy with this plan.

"So, speaking of dinner, shall I cook? I can go to the supermarket?" I said.

"We can order Chinese food for tonight, if you like? Or pizza? My treat," Robert said. "And then we can all go to the store tomorrow and get what we need for the rest of the week?"

"Fine by me."

We settled on pizza, and Diane placed the order, using Robert's credit card.

"I ordered four," she said.

"Four! There are only three of us." I laughed.

"Well, we can eat any leftovers for breakfast."

I shuddered and glanced at Robert to see his reaction, and for the first time since we met, he smiled.

We ate the pizza at the dining table, and I found myself eating much more than I had in days.

Getting to know each other was bitter sweet. Any laughter was soured with immense sadness which always seemed ready to pounce when least expected.

After dinner, Robert fetched his briefcase and took out a manila folder. "Are you sure you want to be present, Princess?"

Diane nodded.

"Okay, then." He cleared his throat. "Basically, the will is divided into three parts. The property—the business—and you, Diane."

I gulped. All my senses lit up, and I wished I hadn't eaten that last slice of pizza.

"The property also includes the house and all the assets. And that's pretty straight forward. Everything is to be sold, and the proceeds will be split into two. Half will go to Diane's carer—there will be more than enough money to support Diane until she's twenty-five years of age. The other half will go into a trust for Diane, which will mature when she's twenty-five."

I nodded taking it all in.

Diane didn't say a word. I couldn't read her expression.

"Eddie set up an insurance policy to pay out the value of the business into their assets fund upon his death. The business itself will go to me, unless anybody wishes to contest it, of course. Eddie was the majority shareholder and with me already being in the company, I guess they felt it was the most logical decision."

"And finally, me," Diane said. "I don't care about the business. What did they want for me?"

Robert swallowed hard. "They want you to take over responsibility of Diane."

I realised he was staring at me.

"Me?"

He nodded.

Diane stared at me wide-eyed. "Say something, then."

I shook myself. "I-I have no problem with that. I'd love you to come and live with me."

"In Manchester?"

"Listen, Diane. My life has been up in the air since Giles died. Let's not make any hard and fast decisions right now. How about we play it by ear?"

"I'd like that."

"And that's it." Robert placed the folder back in his case. "Apart from a lot of smaller, more personal things."

"Like what?" Diane asked.

"Like, your mum wants your aunt to have their parents' dinner service and several other items along the same lines. She wanted you, Diane, to have all her personal jewellery as well as anything else of hers you would want to keep. The rest will be sold or donated to charity."

CHAPTER 12

Diane called Andre's mother again before bed, but he still hadn't arrived home.

"Why are they keeping him locked up? He's done nothing wrong," she cried as she hung up the phone.

"I don't know, sweetheart." I was totally exhausted, but I didn't want to be the first to go to bed, still not totally comfortable in Robert's house.

I wondered if Eddie's partner had also been arrested. That reminded me. "Robert, do you know why Eddie was arguing with his business partner?"

"Was he? They were always bickering about something or other."

"No, Diane seems to think it was something rather big—"

"It was," Diane interrupted. "And you do know, Uncle Rob. Dad told you last week when you came over. The night you brought the whisky."

"Oh, that. Yeah, that was all sorted. Nothing to worry about."

"What was it, then?" I pushed, not totally happy with being fobbed off.

"It was a business decision. Something they couldn't agree on. It happens all the time in business."

Something in the way he spoke to me got my back up. It was as though he was insinuating that I wouldn't understand because I was just a woman. "Well, Giles owned a huge international company and I helped him run it, so I do know how big decisions can cause conflict with the staff. Diane seems to think it was more than that. That in fact Eddie was extremely upset by whatever it was."

"Nothing to worry about. It was all sorted. I promise you."

Diane yawned. "I'm tired, but I don't think I'll be able to sleep."

"Because you're worrying about Andre?" I asked.

She shook her head.

"Are you worried the man might come back?"

She nodded, her eyes filling with tears once again.

"I'll switch the alarm on, Princess," Robert said. "Don't be worrying. Nothing or nobody will get through it. I promise."

She suddenly gasped. "I didn't turn our alarm on. Dad startled me and so I ran upstairs. He must've forgotten too."

"Easy mistake, sweetie," I said.

"No. You don't understand. Dad was obsessed with setting the alarm. If I'd been home on time, it would've been set as usual and nobody would've got in. So that means I'm to blame for their deaths."

"It's not your fault," I said, pulling her into my arms.

Robert hovered at the side of us, clearly uncomfortable.

"But it is. Don't you see?"

"Nonsense. Your dad was quite capable of locking up after you. It was his job to make sure his family was safe and setting the alarm is part of that. And we still don't even know if your dad invited the guy inside. He could've known him."

She stopped crying and glanced up at me. "You think it's someone who knows us?"

"I honestly don't know, sweetie. But what I do know is you're not to blame. Not at all. Now, come on. It's late. Shall we call it a day?"

Sniffing, she nodded and wiped her nose on her arm. Most of the time, she acted older than her age, but when she did things like that it reminded me she was just a little girl really.

"I need to grab my suitcase from the car," I said. "I'll be up in a tick."

"Shall I get it for you?" Robert asked.

This surprised me. It was the first time I felt that he actually didn't mind me being there. I almost said no. Old habits die hard, and I'd never been one to allow men to treat me like the little lady. But I didn't want to offend him seeing as he was making an effort. "That's very nice of you, Robert. Thank you."

"Go on up with Diane if you like. I'm worried about her, but you seem to keep her grounded, thank goodness. I'm grateful to you for agreeing to stay here. I know it's not ideal."

I smiled, genuinely this time. "Thanks, Robert. That means a lot."

I climbed the stairs and bumped into Diane as she came out of the bathroom dressed in black pyjamas. "You okay?" I asked.

She nodded.

"Would you like me to come in with you, see you settled down?"

She shrugged, but her eyes told me that's exactly what she wanted.

"Come on. Let's tuck you in."

I followed her into the room, and she climbed into the three-quarter sized bed.

I sat beside her and stroked her hair. "What made you get rid of your beautiful dark curls?"

"How do you know I had dark curls?"

"Because I saw them. Don't you remember meeting me?"

"Kinda. But I didn't know you'd remember me."

"You're joking, aren't you? You made a huge impression on me. Now come on. Tell me. Why did you ruin your lovely hair?"

"I don't know. Maybe because it got a reaction from my parents."

"You did it just to wind them up?"

She nodded sadly. "I drove them mad."

"Do you even like your hair like this?"

She grinned. "Not really."

The door banged open, and Robert appeared with my case. "Good," he said, nodding at Diane. "I'll take you to the shop for a dye—just say the word." He turned to me. "Where do you want these? In the spare room or are you staying in here?"

"The spare room, I think. It's only next door, isn't it?"

Diane nodded.

"Okay. Goodnight, beautiful girl," I said, automatically, just like my mum used to say to us.

Diane blinked back tears.

"What did I say?"

"Nothing. You just sound so much like her."

I kissed her forehead. "It will get easier, you know? I promise."

"Goodnight, Aunt Susie."

"Goodnight, beautiful girl," I said again.

Robert had left when I turned around, and I found my case on the bed in the spare room. Quickly grabbing a nightie and my toiletry bag, I checked the bathroom was empty before ducking inside to wash my face and brush my teeth. Robert's bedroom door was closed. I didn't know whether to turn the landing light off, so I left it on.

I climbed into the bed, and was impressed by the quality of the fabric. In fact, I couldn't fault anything, and I was quite particular in my own choices.

I sank into the mattress and pillow as though lying on a fluffy cloud. I didn't even bother with my book—sleep was calling and I didn't intend to keep it waiting.

PIERCING screams jolted me from my dream, and my heart thudded in my chest. It took a few seconds to realise where I was and that the screams must be Diane.

I flew from the bed as fast as humanly possible on weak and trembling legs.

Diane was sitting up in bed howling like an injured animal. She was repeating something I couldn't quite make out.

"Shush, sweetie. It was just a dream. It's okay. I'm here."

The fight suddenly left her and she turned limp in my arms sobbing hysterically.

Robert popped his head around the door. "Is she okay?" he whispered. His pained expression made me feel sorry for him. For all that I didn't like the man, he clearly adored Diane.

"She's fine," I mouthed, and offered him a smile.

He nodded and backed out of the room.

After a few minutes, Diane's breathing steadied, but I couldn't bear to leave her. Instead, I climbed in beside her.

As I drifted off to sleep, thoughts of Robert once again occupied my mind. He was an odd nut to crack that's for sure. He'd been standoffish to me since I arrived, but then, on the odd occasion he showed a tender, caring side, especially where Diane was concerned. I drifted off to sleep wondering what his wife must've been like.

CHAPTER 13

I OPENED MY EYES AND WINCED. A SHAFT OF LIGHT POURED IN through a gap in the curtains and had landed across my face.

"Oh, hello," Diane said, opening her eyes.

I smiled. "How are you feeling?"

"Better. Sorry about last night. I could've sworn he was standing over me."

"I can assure you there was nobody here."

"Thanks for staying with me. I feel like I remembered something."

"Really? Something about the man?"

She closed her eyes. "I think so. But it's…" She shook her head, "…it's gone."

"Hopefully it'll come back to you. Let's go and make some breakfast. Distraction is often the way forward with this kind of thing."

We trudged downstairs in our dressing gowns. Robert must've been up as the alarm was turned off, but he was nowhere to be seen.

"Good morning!"

I spun around as an older woman with a ruddy complexion

and bright red cheeks flounced into the kitchen. "Coffee?" she said.

"Yes, please." I glanced at Diane who was nosing in the kitchen cupboard.

"Cinnamon, this is my Aunt Susie."

The woman grasped hold of my hand shaking it heartily. "Lovely to meet you."

"And you."

"I'm Robert's housekeeper. He told me to let you know the vicar will be calling in this afternoon."

The doorbell rang putting both me and Diane in a panic with us still being in our nightwear.

"Don't worry. I'll get it," Cinnamon said, heading to the door.

"Shall we go and get dressed?" I asked.

Diane nodded and we ran to the stairs giggling.

"DI Jenkins. Could I speak to Ms Carmichael and Miss Hewitt, please?" We heard as we made it up to the landing.

"Be quick," I said, rushing into the bathroom where I brushed my teeth and cleaned my face on a makeup wipe. I figured I could always have a shower later.

Diane was dressed in a pair of hip-hugging black jeans and a long-sleeved black T-shirt. She was standing outside the bathroom door when I ran out.

I quickly dressed and applied a swipe of eyeliner and dabbed a touch of lipstick to my lips.

"Ready?" I asked Diane moments later.

"Gosh, look at you. How did you manage to look so good in such a short time?" she said, incredulously.

"Practice. Come on." I held out my hand, and we walked downstairs together.

"Sorry to call in unannounced, ladies," Conrad said, as we entered, getting to his feet.

I caught a faint whiff of his citrusy aftershave. "That's okay. What can we do for you?"

He shook our hands before returning to the two-seater sofa.

"I called in at the hotel, but Ryan told me you'd checked out."

"Yeah. Diane wanted me to stay here."

"Why did you arrest Andre?" Diane said, unable to hold back any longer.

"Ah, jungle drums." He grinned.

"What are you even on about?" she sneered.

"Be nice." I eyeballed my outspoken niece.

"We did take Mr Cooper in for questioning. I don't think he had anything to do with the case."

"I could've told you that. I told you what the guy looked like."

"No, you told us he was a smaller build than your dad, and he wore a grey T-shirt."

"He had a cough."

My head snapped around to stare at Diane.

"I remembered," she said to me. "I had a dream last night, and I thought he'd come back for me. He had a cough and I think maybe a limp, because when I heard him walking upstairs he sounded like he was dragging his foot." Diane got to her feet and acted out what she'd heard. Clomp… scrape. Clomp… scrape.

"That's a great help, Diane," Conrad said.

"Did you question Eddie's business partner?" I asked.

"No. It seems Donald Macy is in Portugal on holiday. He's not due back for another week."

"I mentioned the fight to Robert last night," I said. "He told us that Eddie and Donald had a little misunderstanding, but he didn't seem to think it was anything out of the ordinary. We also discovered Robert is set to inherit the business."

Conrad's eyebrows arched deliciously. "Really?"

I nodded pleased my silent message hadn't been lost on him.

"Is Mr Hewitt around? I wouldn't mind having a word with him."

"No, sorry. We don't know where he is, but I'm sure he won't be long. Can I get you a coffee? I was just about to make one."

"That would be nice, thanks."

"Do you need me for anything else?" Diane said. "I want to go and phone Andre."

"That's all for now, Diane. Thanks."

She gave him a backward nod and headed upstairs.

"Come through to the kitchen?"

The housekeeper had already made a pot of coffee. I poured two cups. "Milk and sugar?"

"A splash of milk, thanks."

I handed him his coffee, and we settled on two stools beside the island. I clocked him glancing around the stunning kitchen.

"Nice, isn't it?" I asked.

"I'll say."

"Not what I was expecting at all. It's almost as flash as my sister's place." I took a sip of my coffee and placed it back on the countertop.

"That reminds me. The SOCO team have finished in your sister's house. You will want to arrange for a cleaner to get in there before you allow Diane back in.

I shuddered. "I don't know if she'd want to go back in, to be honest. I'm not even sure I could."

"Understandable." He sipped the coffee and wiped his moustache down with his fingers.

"So, have you got any closer to finding out what happened?"

He shook his head. "Quite a lot of blood was found on and around the sink in the bathroom, so we know the killer had a good wash before leaving."

"How, though? Diane said she heard him kill her mum and then he headed downstairs for her."

"She was in shock. The timeline can't be relied on unfortunately."

"Yeah, I thought that. I mean, if he was in the room with Diane as the police arrived, why did nobody see anything?"

"Exactly. She may have blanked out well before my guys arrived giving him enough time to get away."

"And this new info—the cough and the limp? Does that help at all?"

"Not at this stage, but we'll definitely bear it in mind. I do need to ask you if you have anyone who can verify your whereabouts on the night of the murders."

I almost choked on my coffee. "You're kidding, right?"

"It's simply for the record. I wouldn't be doing my job properly if I didn't check into every single scenario."

"Then I guess you'd better arrest me as I have no alibi. I got home from the airport and crashed for most of the day and night."

"How about CCTV? Do you know if they have any cameras at your apartment?"

"I'd say so. It's pretty up to date with everything else."

"Thanks for that. I'll contact the security firm, and that should be enough to cross you off the list."

"I can't believe I'm on it, to be honest."

"In this game, you learn to treat everyone as a potential suspect. I'm sorry if I've upset you. That wasn't my intention."

"I understand." I heard the judder of the garage door. "Robert's here," I said, and drained my mug just as Robert appeared in the hallway.

"Good morning, Mr Hewitt," Conrad said, getting to his feet and extending his hand.

"Oh, hi. I wondered whose car was parked skew-whiff in the street."

Conrad barked out a laugh. "Yeah, that's me. Parking has never been my thing, I'm afraid."

"That's a first," I said, highly amused. "I thought it was just women who couldn't parallel park."

"Just women and one man."

I rolled my eyes. "I'll leave you guys to it," I said and headed for the stairs.

Diane had obviously got hold of her boyfriend as I could hear her talking ten to the dozen in her bedroom.

I lay down on my bed and I read a few pages of my Kindle. I was unsure what the rest of the day held. The housekeeper had mentioned the vicar, but I didn't think the bodies had been released yet, so it seemed a little premature to start organising funerals in my opinion.

A few minutes later, I heard Conrad leave.

CHAPTER 14

Diane knocked and popped her head around my bedroom door a few minutes later. "Is it okay if Andre comes over?"

"It's okay by me, but it's not my house. Maybe ask your uncle." I swivelled around and put my feet on the floor placing my Kindle on the bedside table.

Her eyes were morose and filled with disappointment. "He'll say no. He's a dick."

"Hey. That's not nice. Maybe we could ask him together? What do you think?"

"We can try."

We found Robert in his office, which was the door next to the garage.

"Uncle Rob," Diane said, her fingers crossed.

"Uh-huh."

"Is it okay if Andre comes around for a little while?"

His head snapped up, and he scowled. "No way. He's just spent the night in the nick being questioned for murder."

"He didn't do it, though. That Detective said as much. Didn't he, Aunt Susie?"

Robert's head snapped up again clearly surprised to find me

standing in the doorway. "I don't care what the Detective said. I don't want him in my house sizing everything up, waiting for the opportunity to help himself."

"Fuck you. He's not a thief, and you know it."

"Come on, Diane. Let's leave it now."

"No. Tell him. He's being a tosser."

Robert waved her words away and turned back to his computer.

I grabbed Diane's hand and shook my head placing a finger to my lips.

She followed me out.

"You're not going to get him to change his mind by being an obnoxious teenager."

"But he was being horrid. Andre has a few piercings and dyes his hair black. It doesn't make him a criminal."

"Shall we pop around to see him instead this time? I'd like to meet him, and then I'll have a word with Robert privately and see if I can change his mind."

Her eyes widened as she looked at me hopefully. "You wouldn't mind? You can meet his mum too. She's dope." She pulled out her phone and began tapping away, her fingers flying over the keypad.

"Are we taking the car?" I asked as we stepped from the house, pulling the front door closed behind us.

"It's not far, but it's up to you."

"Let's walk."

Diane slid her arm through mine, and we set off at a brisk pace.

"How long has Andre been your boyfriend?" I asked, after we'd been walking a few minutes.

"We've been friends for two years, but I only started seeing him a couple of months ago."

"But your parents didn't approve?"

She screwed her face up. "You've seen first-hand how controlling Dad was with Mum, triple it and add a hundred. Now ask yourself if he'd like any boy who showed an interest in his only child."

"But it sounds like you chose the most undesirable person you could find. Was that just to make a point?"

She grinned. "At first, maybe. But Andre is lovely, and he treats me like a queen. If you look past the whole goth thing, I'm sure you'll like him."

We turned the corner and crossed the road.

"I'll give him a fair shot at getting me onside. Lord knows you need your friends around you right now."

"You're cool, Aunt Susie. I'm just sad I can't remember what you and Mum were like together."

I smiled, my mind wandering to a time before Eddie. "Your mum and I fought like cat and dog growing up, but we were best friends most of the time. I miss her."

"Me too. Although I can't remember the last time we enjoyed each other's company. Mum defended Dad all the time, and I felt as though they were both against me. Like they wanted me to be miserable for the rest of my life."

"You know that's not true, don't you? Being a parent must be a nightmare. Everybody has a different take on it, and there are no hard and fast rules." We strolled past a playground. "Look at all the parents over there. What do they all have in common?"

She shrugged. "Dunno."

"Look at their faces. Each one of them is on edge like standing on guard waiting for something awful to happen. It's like a perpetual feeling of doom descends on a person when they become parents."

She glanced at each of them, her eyebrows furrowed.

"You've got to know your parents only wanted the best for you."

"I know they did. Is that why you never had kids?"

"I'd like to say yes, and that I'd never wanted kids of my own, but it's not true."

"So, you do want them?"

I shrugged. "I did. Probably too late for me now."

"What happened? Why didn't you?"

"I did. I had four, in total. Three boys and a girl. But none of them went full term."

Diane gasped and gripped my arm tightly.

"The longest any of them lived was three days—baby Jack. Sharon, Sam and Russel each lived for a few hours only."

"That's terrible. Did Mum know?"

"She knew about Sharon. She was my first born. But I didn't tell anybody after that. I wanted to wait until my pregnancies had reached the third trimester. It sounds silly, but I wanted to spare everybody else the pain and grief."

"You told nobody at all?"

"Just Giles. I kept it from my parents. I couldn't bear seeing them lose another grandchild. It was easier for me to cope with the loss when fewer people knew."

Diane stopped walking and nodded at a tidy semi-detached house, with a small front garden. "We're here, but I don't want to go in yet. I want to hear all about my cousins. I'm so sorry, Aunt Susie."

"It's okay. We've got plenty of time to talk. In fact, this is the first time I've ever spoken about them."

"Ever?"

I nodded my head sadly. "It was easier that way."

The front door opened, and a lanky young man dressed in typical goth attire, with a shock of black hair and pockmarked skin, stepped onto the doorstep.

I smiled up at him and followed Diane up the steps towards him.

Diane introduced us.

"Nice to meet you," Andre said, politely.

I gasped when I noticed the huge hole in one of the boy's earlobes.

Diane laughed. A pleasant tinkling sound that I hadn't heard over the past few days.

Andre invited us inside, and I weighed up the neat and tidy home, nothing extraordinary but homely and clean. Apart from the piercings, I hadn't seen anything that explained why Steph and Eddie were so against them seeing each other.

"Diane," a woman with straight, brown, shoulder-length hair marched down the hallway towards us, her arms outstretched. She was dressed in black slacks and a white blouse. "I know I've already said it over the phone, but I want to tell you how utterly devastated I am for you."

"Thanks, Mrs Cooper," Diane hugged her back.

"Now, you must be Diane's aunt. She's been telling me all about you." The woman took my hand and pumped it enthusiastically. I liked her instantly.

"Really?" I smiled at Diane and then turned back to the woman.

"Don't worry. It was all good. I'm Teresa Cooper, Andre's mum. Come on through. I'll make us a cuppa. Unless you fancy a glass of wine? It's 4pm somewhere in the world."

"Coffee's fine for me, thanks. But don't let me stop you."

"I couldn't possibly drink alone—what would you think of me?" She chuckled steering me towards the back of the house and through to the compact kitchen.

Diane and Andre didn't come with us, and I was a little disappointed. I'd wanted the chance to form my own opinions of the boy.

"Sugar and milk?" Teresa asked.

"Just a drop of milk, please."

"So, how long are you staying for? I believe you live abroad."

"My main home is in Manchester, but I have a small villa in Spain where I've spent the summer."

"Nice. I've been planning to take Andre on holiday, but it's difficult enough to find the money to keep this place afloat since my husband walked out."

"I'm sorry. That's tough."

She waved my words away. "Ignore me. I have a nasty habit of saying exactly what's on my mind when I'm nervous."

"Why are you nervous?"

"I'm not used to visitors—especially ones who live abroad."

"You're nervous of me?" I asked, shaking my head in surprise.

"Don't look at me like that!" She grinned. "Just look at you. You're gorgeous."

"So are you, silly."

"Yeah, right. I wore my interview clothes when I found out you were coming over, and I had to drag out the cups that have the least chips in them."

Her honesty was refreshing.

CHAPTER 15

As I predicted, Teresa and I got on like a house on fire, and by the end of the visit we were firm friends.

"Do come again," she urged, hugging me.

"I will but only if you promise no airs and graces."

"Deal."

I turned to see Andre kiss Diane on the lips. Raising my eyebrows, I glanced at Teresa. "Oops."

Teresa smiled. "Put the poor girl down, Andre."

Andre turned several shades of red and took a step back from Diane.

"So, what did you think?" Diane asked once we were alone again and heading back to Robert's.

"I didn't get to see very much of Andre, but what I did see I liked. His mum's lovely."

"Dad couldn't stand her. He said she's got mental issues."

"Haven't we all," I said. I wanted to tell her, her dad was a control freak mental case, but how could I? He was her dad, and he was dead.

"What did you talk about?"

"Just stuff. She told me her husband had left her."

"Yeah. Andre was gutted when he went. There was no warning. He just didn't come home from work one day. Sent a text telling her he'd met someone else, and that was it. He's still not been in touch with Andre, and it was over six months ago."

"Bloody hell. That's terrible."

The sky had turned dark and moody, and a grumble of thunder made me shiver.

"Do you think we'll make it home before it pees down?" I asked.

"Let's run."

I tried to keep up with Diane, but she soon sped off in front—much fitter than I was. I kept her in my sights not certain which way we'd walked earlier.

She was sitting on the doorstep grinning at me when I turned into Robert's driveway a few minutes later.

Fat drops of rain splashed on the concrete, and the sky lit up followed by a loud growl of thunder above us.

I jumped onto the doorstep beside her, and Diane rang the bell.

Robert opened the door and walked away back to his office without saying a word—clearly still in a mood.

I winced at Diane who just shrugged.

"Tosser," she mouthed.

I smiled despite the fact I was probably meant to give her a telling off for saying such a thing about her uncle. But I happened to agree with her. He was a tosser.

"I've arranged for cleaners to go through Eddie's place," Robert threw over his shoulder. "Oh, and you missed the vicar. He came to discuss the funeral."

"So that's it?" Diane said, on the verge of tears. "We can't have a say in the funeral?"

"What do you take me for, Diane? Of course, I told him he'd have to return another day. But he wasn't very happy to have his time wasted."

Diane glanced at me.

"Tosser," I mouthed.

She slammed her hand to her mouth and snorted.

We went through to the kitchen, and I made us both a ham sandwich. I contemplated making one for Robert, but I felt funny offering him his own food.

"After lunch, shall we go to the supermarket? I can make something for dinner," I said.

Diane didn't answer. She stared from the kitchen window to the cluster of trees and low hanging branches at the end of the garden.

"Does the garden back directly onto your garden?" I asked.

She didn't appear to hear me.

"Did you hear what he said about the cleaners, Aunt Susie?"

I nodded.

"The police must've finished in there, then."

"Yes. The Detective mentioned it this morning. But don't worry. You don't need to go back in there, unless you want to, that is."

"How would you feel about going in there?"

I gulped. "I will if you want me to. Why?"

"I was thinking maybe we should stay there. I can't stand Uncle Rob when he gets in a snit like this."

"You did call him a tosser earlier."

"So did you."

"Yeah, but not to his face. Would you rather have to go back home or swallow your pride and apologise? You know he's a pushover where you're concerned."

She lifted one shoulder and held it against her chin before letting it drop. "We can't stay here forever, though. Maybe we should just go back for a visit. See how we feel once we're inside."

"Well, if you're sure," I said, my stomach doing somersaults "but can we wait until the cleaners have been? It will be difficult enough without having to face the…"

"Blood?" she said. "You can say it, you know."

I rolled my eyes. "I just didn't want to upset you."

"I know. Sorry to be such a bitch."

"You're not. It's okay. Come and get your sandwich."

"What should we do for dinner then?" She came to sit beside me at the breakfast bar.

"I don't even know what you like to eat. What's your favourite?" I took a bite from my sandwich, suddenly ravenous.

"I love all the kid things."

"Kid things?" I shook my head.

"Yeah. Pizza, burgers, kebabs—all fast food."

I shuddered. "Is that all? What did your mum make for you? I can't imagine her letting you have too much fast food. She used to be a food snob."

"She didn't mind what I had so long as half my plate was filled with vegetables."

"Ah, that's how you got around it?"

"Yeah. I hate vegetables."

"Then why tell me what she used to make you do?" I grinned. "You know I'll feel obliged to do the same now."

She winced. "I realised that as the words left my mouth. Can't we just rewind and pretend you didn't hear it?"

"No can do, I'm afraid. Finish your sandwich—we need to go vegetable shopping."

She groaned and tossed the last bite of her sandwich into her mouth.

CHAPTER 16

We settled on making homemade burgers and Robert joined us for dinner. Diane, to her credit, apologised to him, and he seemed relieved. He opened a bottle of red wine and insisted I shared it with him.

"Pile the salad on your plate." I eyeballed Diane.

She scowled at me, good-naturedly.

Robert just glanced at us and shook his head, clearly not interested in what we were on about, and I had no intention letting him know.

"Did the cleaners finish at the house?" Diane asked.

"I think so. They didn't contact me with any problems, so I guess it's done. I'll check it out later. I need to set the alarm anyway. Why do you want to know?"

"I want to go around tomorrow. I'm hoping it jolts my memory."

"I'll go over with you in the afternoon," he said. "I have a meeting in the morning I can't get out of."

"No, it's okay. Aunt Susie will come with me."

He bit his lip and ran a jerky hand through his hair. "I'm not sure that's a good idea. It will be traumatic."

"I know that. But we'll be fine. Won't we?" She glanced at me with raised eyebrows.

Although not convinced, I refused to be on Robert's side. Something about him rubbed me up the wrong way. "I hope so. I guess we'll find out in the morning."

ONCE AGAIN, Diane woke up screaming in the early hours.

Robert didn't even bother getting up to check on her this time, and I silently slid into the bed beside her and stroked her hair until she drifted off into an unsettled slumber.

The next morning, I woke and showered while Diane was still sound asleep. I applied makeup and, for the first time in months, I straightened my frizzy blonde hair. I was surprised how different I not only looked but felt, as though I'd applied a full set of body armour.

"You look nice," Diane said, appearing behind me in the kitchen.

"Thought I'd make an effort. What do you fancy for breakfast?"

"I don't know if I want anything. I'm sorry about last night. You must be getting sick of me."

"Don't be silly, sweetie." I placed the coffee container on the side and pulled her into my arms. "It's going to take time, that's all."

"Do you still want to go to the house?" She looked up at me, expectantly.

"Do you?"

She nodded, but I could see the fear behind her eyes.

"We'll just go and play it by ear. If you want to leave at any time, just say."

"Okay."

"Get dressed then." I shoved her towards the doorway playfully.

I ate a slice of toast and downed two cups of coffee trying to prepare myself mentally and physically. I needed to be Diane's rock.

Instead of walking to the bottom of the garden and through to the back of my sister's house, Diane suggested we go in the car.

My heart raced as we pulled into the driveway. I glanced at Diane whose huge blue eyes stared at the imposing house.

"Are you ready? We don't have to do this."

She shook her head. "No, it's fine. But it's strange. I thought I would be terrified, but it just looks like home."

"It's still your home. You had a lot of fantastic memories here that can't be wiped out by one terrible one."

She blew out a steady breath and nodded. "I know."

"But if you're not ready don't go inside. I can get your stuff if you'd prefer." I made the offer without thinking, but the thought of going inside alone was enough to have me running for the hills.

She unbuckled her seatbelt. "No, we can do this. I just wish I'd asked Andre to come too."

"We don't need Andre. We make a formidable team—just the two of us." That familiar stomach twirl once again belied my confident words.

We got out of the car, and I waited for her to come around to me before I held my hand out.

She grabbed it with both of hers.

Although cold, the August sun had made an appearance, teasing us. It was the height of summer, and yet it felt more like winter. But that wasn't the cause of the shivers I suddenly felt as we approached the front door.

"Do you have a key?" I asked.

She nodded digging into her jacket pocket and pulling out a small blue purse with a key dangling from it. Her trembling fingers fumbled at the lock, so I took the key from her, and opened the door. A series of beeps tore at my already jangling nerves.

Diane rushed to a box on the wall and punched in several numbers silencing the beeps.

Feeling lightheaded, I thought I was likely to flake out at any minute.

A strange scent assaulted my nose, cloying and pungent, like someone had tried to mask an underlying stench.

I smiled at Diane wanting to be guided by her.

"What's that stink?" she said, gripping her nose.

"The cleaners, no doubt."

"It's disgusting like rotten flower petals."

I couldn't have described it better myself. The cloying stench was giving me a headache. "Maybe we should open the doors and windows while we're here." I let go of her hand and opened the door wide placing a large clown doorstop behind it so it wouldn't swing closed.

With a mission in mind, I took control and marched through to the grand living room. Three tan leather sofas had been placed around a coffee table. I opened the cream vertical blinds and the windows beyond them allowing the sun to pour into the room. It was a nice room, I told myself. Immaculate, just like I remembered, and not in the least bit scary.

CHAPTER 17

"You okay?" I asked, turning back to Diane.

She perched on the edge of the sofa closest to the door. "I am. But can we stay in here for a sec?"

"Of course, we can, sweetie." I sat beside her glad of the brief pause. It enabled me to get a feel for the house. I glanced around at the meagre furnishings. Steph had always been a minimalist. The only personal item I could see was one of Steph and Eddie's wedding photos, in a solid silver frame beside a lamp on the side table. Other than that, there was nothing to tell me anything about the people who once lived there.

"That's a huge TV," I said, shocked at the size of the screen that almost covered the entire wall.

"Dad had to have the best technology available. It's a sixty-five inch smart TV."

"I won't pretend to understand what you mean, but I didn't think your mum even watched TV."

"She didn't. Dad didn't often, either."

"Then why such a whopper?" I shook my head confused. My TV in the Manchester apartment was a quarter of the size, and it did nothing but connect to half a dozen channels—more than enough, in my opinion. I didn't even own a TV in the villa.

"You knew Dad. Technology snob."

"I guess it's because he worked in technology. I couldn't care less about that kind of thing," I said.

"Me neither."

"So, what shall we do? Check out the kitchen?"

She nodded.

"If you see anything missing, point it out. Even though the police don't seem to think it was a robbery, they don't know the place like you do."

We walked hand in hand into the kitchen. It was huge. Much bigger than I remembered with a large utility room off the main room. The white marble worktops were clear of clutter. Everything you would usually find on display in a kitchen was hidden from sight in the utility room, including the kettle and coffee maker. All the units were white high gloss. The only splash of colour, if you could call black a colour, was the double-sized range cooker. Even the floor tiles were spotless white.

I glanced in the fridge and realised there were a lot of things that needed throwing away before they started to stink. But I'd worry about that another time.

"Did your mum have a cleaner too?" I asked, remembering Steph's untidy bedroom as a child.

"No. She was OCD about cleaning. She did the whole house every single day."

"That's not something that was passed down through the genes." I smiled. "I hate cleaning."

"Same."

"Having nothing on the worktops reminds me of an empty house."

"I know. Everyone says that. I'm used to it now. The only room with clutter in it is my bedroom, and that drove Mum bananas. She hated going in there."

"I shouldn't tell tales, seeing as she's not here to defend herself, but your mum's room used to be the pits. She never hung her clothes up—they lived on a chair in the corner. She would start searching for something and within seconds, you couldn't see a patch of carpet for clothes. Our mum refused to go in there."

Diane shook her head, wide-eyed. "I wish I knew that before. She always went on about how her mum wouldn't stand for mess and I didn't know how lucky I was to have such easy-going parents."

I snorted. "She was still a good storyteller then. My parents used to call her Bette Davis because of her acting skills. She'd convince anybody of anything with her porkies."

"Porkies?"

"Porky pies, lies."

Diane's face lit up, and she smiled. "I can't imagine her as a kid. Do you have any photos?"

"Loads. They're in storage in Manchester, but I can get hold of them easily enough."

"I'd like that."

"When does school start again?"

"I think two weeks on Monday." Her face dropped as she spoke.

"What?"

"I don't want to go back to school."

"You've got no choice, I'm afraid, madam. It's the law."

She shrugged. "Shall we get this over with? I don't feel as bad down here as I thought I would."

"Good. I don't either, to be honest." I opened the back door and a gust of wind blasted in. "Maybe I'll keep that closed." I slammed it shut, feeling windswept.

The next room we went into was the plush office. A heavy oak desk took up the bulk of the room. Huge, black and white abstract art work was on each wall. On the way out, I noticed the lock had been broken, and I remembered this was where Diane had been when she made the call to the police.

"Are you okay?"

She nodded. "It seems like a bad dream, now."

"Do you remember anything else?"

"No. Nothing."

"Shall we call it a day?"

"No. Unless you want to, that is?"

I shook my head. "I'm fine."

We set off up the wide, sweeping staircase. As the stairs turned, I noticed the first dark, wet patch, and felt the moisture in the air. The cloying, sickly stink was stronger up there too. "Is that…?" I pointed to the carpet and remembered that was where she found her dad's dead body.

Her nails dug into the flesh of my hand. She nodded, skirting around it, her eyes full of tears. The first of the day, which was surprising considering what we were actually doing.

"He lay there…" she said, with trembling lips. "…his head pointed down the stairs, his body twisted. One leg was under him, but the other was stretched out and must've kicked the hallstand and the vase over." Tears ran freely down her cheeks now. She didn't even try to wipe them clearly reliving the moment.

I nodded not wanting to jolt her from her memory. I hoped she'd remember something that could help Conrad find the bastard who'd done this to our family.

She eventually continued up the stairs, walked along the wide landing and stopped at the first door on the left. A sob caught in her throat, and she turned and buried her face in my neck.

Once again, the cleaners had done a fantastic job removing the blood. A faint stain the size of a rubbish bin lid was on the carpet beside the bed.

It suddenly struck me. All the time I was trying to stay strong for Diane, I'd completely blocked it out of my mind that this affected me too. This was the exact spot my sister lost her life. The stain was where her life's blood had poured from her fatal stab wound.

Without warning, I crumpled to the carpet and sobbed, briefly forgetting all about my niece and the effect my reaction would be having on her. But I needn't have worried—Diane seemed to be coping better than I was. She stroked my hair until I gained some kind of control.

After a few minutes, we got to our feet and sat on the bed.

I glanced around my sister's bedroom at the high quality white tall boy and matching dressing table, all still clutter free. Even the bedside cabinets had nothing on top apart from a lamp on each and a small clock on the far side of the bed.

"Still nothing?" I asked.

"No. Mum was kneeling beside the bed here, and I saw just the back of him in the mirror there. He must've been standing here." Renewed tears poured down her cheeks as she spoke. She got to her feet and stood a couple of feet away from where Steph would have been.

"It's awful. I'm sorry for my meltdown," I said. "It's just all too much to take in."

"Do you think you'd be able to stay here?" Her hopeful eyes sought out mine.

"Do you still want to?"

She nodded. "I want to feel close to them. But if it's too much for you, then I understand."

"I'll make a deal with you. We will arrange for the carpet to be replaced in here and on the landing and stairs, and then we'll arrange to move back in. How does that sound?"

"Okay."

"Come on then. Let's go and organise it." I held my hand out for her, and we headed downstairs sidestepping the stains.

CHAPTER 18

Robert was furious when I told him of our plans. Diane had gone upstairs to call Andre, and I thought it was best I told him without her input.

"You must be off your rocker! Why the hell would you want to stay there after everything that's happened?"

"Because Diane wants to go home. She's lost too much, and if I can help her form some semblance of order then I will. Surely you understand that?"

"I understand that you're enabling her. She's the child and you're the adult here—don't forget that."

"What's that supposed to mean?"

"I mean…" He paused as though trying to calm himself down and find the correct words. "I mean, you really don't know Diane. You're playacting being a parent. I'm not knocking it. In fact I think it's a credit to you, but you don't know the trouble she caused for Eddie and Steph."

"I can imagine. That girl has a fire in her belly and a brain in her head. She's not the type to be dictated to and moulded into another sheep. So, yes, I can imagine it didn't go down too well with your control freak brother."

His eyes shot fire at me as he wiped his mouth with a napkin, threw it down onto his empty plate, and stormed from the room. Just as I thought he'd gone, he reappeared startling me out of my skin. "You actually have no fucking idea," he spat before leaving again. This time he slammed the garage door shut behind him, and I heard the roller door judder into life.

"What was that all about?" Diane padded down the stairs, her phone still held to her ear.

"Oh, your uncle is angry with our decision."

"But we will still do it, won't we? I really want to go home, Aunt Susie." Diane chewed on the inside of her cheek, pleading with her eyes.

"Yes. I said we would, didn't I?"

She grinned and headed up the stairs chattering away incessantly like only a teenage girl can.

"Do you want to get in with me tonight?" I asked Diane as we got ready for bed.

"Would you mind?"

"Of course I don't mind, silly. Let's face it, my bed's bigger than yours so we might get a decent night's sleep."

"I'd like that, then."

"What about setting the alarm? Do you know the number?"

Diane shook her head. "Mum told me once, but I can't remember it."

"Hopefully, he'll be back before too long," I said, with a smile, but I felt a little uneasy going to bed without the protection of the alarm. I was certain this was Robert's way of punishing us for not doing as we were told. He was more like his brother than I'd first thought.

Once Diane was tucked up in my bed, I rammed the handle of

my hairbrush into the gap under the door, then tried the handle. The door wouldn't budge. Satisfied, I climbed in beside her.

"Goodnight, sweetie," I said, turning my back and reaching for my Kindle.

Within moments, Diane began to snore softly.

I sighed, glancing around at her innocent little face. She was such a beautiful girl if only she'd get rid of the Worzel Gummidge hair. But I wouldn't pressure her—she'd see sense before too long.

THE VIOLENT RATTLING of the door handle had me out of bed in a shot. My blood turned to ice. "Who's there?" I called.

Diane began to whimper from the bed.

"Who is it?" I said, much louder this time.

Suddenly the door handle rattled once more.

"Is Diane with you?" Robert's voice boomed through the door.

I yanked the hairbrush out of the gap and pulled the door open. "What the fuck is wrong with you?" I yelled into Robert's surprised face.

"I couldn't find Diane. I thought..." He glanced at Diane, rocking backwards and forwards, tears streaming down her face. "I'm sorry. I didn't think."

"You're telling me you didn't think. I've spent nights trying to calm her down and you hammer on the door in the dead of night like a raving fucking lunatic." I didn't usually swear, but sometimes being polite just didn't cut the mustard.

"I tried to peek in, but your door was locked."

"Do you know how creepy that sounds? Don't ever peek in my room while I'm sleeping, thanks very much."

"Not like that. Listen, I'm sorry. I'll let you get back to bed, and we can talk in the morning."

I slammed the door and replaced the hairbrush. Then I

climbed back onto the bed. "Come here, sweetie. It's alright. He was just worried about you that's all."

"How did he know I wasn't there? He must've been in my room because the door was shut. Maybe it was him I've felt standing over me the last couple of nights?"

Prickles formed at the back of my neck and travelled down my spine. *Could Robert...?* I shook my head trying to remove the thoughts that suddenly invaded my mind. But it was no use. I lay staring at the ceiling for the rest of the night. When dawn finally came around, I got out of bed and grabbed my toiletry bag heading across the hall to the bathroom.

I needed to have an early start. I couldn't bear the thought of spending one more night under Robert's roof. I'd not liked him since we met, but I honestly thought he had Diane's best interests at heart. Now I wasn't so sure. For all that I was nervous of sleeping in Steph's house, I'd rather that than the thought of Robert standing over me and Diane while we slept. Who knows how long it would be before he decided to get rid of us too.

As I stepped from the shower, I cried out in shock. Written in the steam across the huge mirror was:

I'M COMING FOR YOU!

I GRABBED my towel and frantically rubbed the words away, petrified Diane would see them, but, by doing that, I'd cleared away any potential evidence.

Already a nervous wreck, I yelped and my feet left the floor as I emerged from the bathroom to find Robert hovering at my bedroom door.

He jumped too, and a guilty expression crossed his face.

"What are you doing? Didn't you get the message last night? This kind of behaviour is not acceptable, Robert."

"I thought I heard you up. I wanted to talk before I left for work. I've made a pot of coffee."

I eyed him nastily, taking pleasure as he squirmed in his highly-polished shoes. "I'll be down in a few minutes," I said, curtly. I was certain he'd left the mirror message to put us off leaving, but I refused to give him the satisfaction of knowing he'd freaked me out.

I stepped quietly into the bedroom and dropped off my toiletry bag, relieved Diane was still sleeping. She needed to catch up on her rest.

Robert was sitting at the breakfast bar moping over his coffee cup.

He jumped to his feet when he noticed me and proceeded to pour another for me.

I took the coffee and sat opposite him.

"About last night," he said, his cheeks flushing. "I got home late and before locking up wanted to make sure Diane was okay. I panicked when I saw her bed hadn't even been slept in. I didn't think. I just stormed to your room to see if she was there. But the door was locked. I didn't know there was a lock on that door."

"There isn't. I jammed something behind it because you weren't home, and we didn't know how to set the alarm. You know how paranoid that child is after everything. I wasn't about to leave her alone in an unsecured house."

"I'm sorry. I was around at Eddie's house, and I lost track of the time."

"What were you doing there?" I asked suspiciously.

"I pulled up the carpet on the stairs and the master bedroom, ready for you to arrange for somebody to replace it. You'll be glad I did. I couldn't believe the amount of blood congealed underneath the carpet and underlay. It was horrific."

"Oh. Thanks. I didn't think about that."

"I brought you a carpet sample to take to the shop. Hopefully they'll be able to match it."

I felt bad for the thoughts I'd been having about him all night. "I don't get you, Robert. One minute, you're an obnoxious arsehole, and the next you're lovely and thoughtful."

"I'm sorry if I don't know the correct way to behave after losing my only brother. I want to protect Diane, but I feel as though I'm losing her too."

"Only because of your attitude towards her."

"Maybe you're right. But I know how unstable she is. All this nicey niceness she's feeding you is a crock of shit. She made your sister's life hell these past few months."

"Uncle Rob!" Diane squealed from the kitchen doorway.

We both stared at her with gaping mouths. How much had she heard?

"Why would you say that?"

"Because it's true, Princess. Your mum and dad were beside themselves worrying about what to do with you."

"That's a fucking lie!" she screamed.

I jumped to my feet and pulled her into my arms. "Okay, that's enough," I said to them both. I eyeballed Robert. "We are all upset. I think it's quite normal to take our pain out on each other, but it's not what we need right now. Diane, go and get ready, sweetie. We're going to order the carpet. Uncle Robert was good enough to lift the old carpet for us. Weren't you, Robert?"

He nodded, looking down at his now empty mug.

Diane squinted at him before skulking off upstairs.

"Why would you say those things to her?" I hissed.

"Because it's true. Eddie told me just that week she was out of control."

"She's a fifteen-year-old girl, Robert. Kids that age never see eye to eye with their parents. That doesn't make her a bad person. All I see is a very sad little girl. She's admitted she made their lives hell. Don't you think she feels bad enough as it is?"

His shoulders slumped again, and, to my horror, he began crying.

Fuck!

I had no choice but to comfort him. How could I not? I wasn't a callous human being. So, begrudgingly, I walked around the island and put my arms around him. It wasn't his fault he was unlikeable. He *had* lost his brother, and no doubt felt as devastated as I did.

Hearing Diane on the stairs, he stood up, snatched up a tea-towel and strode to the window, his back to the room.

"Ready?" I asked Diane with a smile.

She nodded, her eyes still full of tears.

"Come on, then. I've also got to call into the hotel to pay my bill. It wasn't ready the other day."

"Okay." She got her jacket from the tiny cloakroom beside the front door.

"See you later, Robert," I called, and then remembered the sample. "Oh, hang on there a sec," I said to Diane. I walked back to the kitchen to find Robert splashing his face under the tap. "Where's the sample, Robert?" I asked.

"In the garage. Just inside the door."

"Did you manage to clean up what we discussed earlier? It's just if we go over there, I'd hate for Diane to… you know."

"It's all cleaned up. That's what took so long. I moved the furniture from the bedroom into the spare room, ripped up the carpet and underlay, and then scrubbed the bare wood after that."

"Thanks, Robert."

He nodded. "The vicar has your number. He wants to catch up with you both in the next few days. I won't be here. I need to go to Ireland for a while."

"Ireland?" I asked.

"Yes. I'm going to visit my parents. They're distraught at Eddie's death."

"Of course. Will you leave the alarm number for me?"

"I don't really want to write it down anywhere. Can I show you now?"

I nodded.

Diane gave him a filthy look when he walked towards the front door.

He showed us both the number sequence, and I hoped between us we'd remember it. Otherwise we'd be in a pickle.

"I'll have my phone on me if you have a problem," he said. Then he strode off into his office.

CHAPTER 19

Ryan leaned on the bar and arched one eyebrow when we entered the pub via the internal door from the hotel. "Now, ain't that a sight for sore eyes?" he said.

"Still struggling for staff, I see." I grinned.

"More than ever. You're not looking for a job, are you?"

"What?" I laughed. "Me behind the bar? I'd scare away all your customers."

He tapped a finger on his chin. "Hmmm, fair point. We do need a chambermaid."

Diane snorted. "He only wants to see you in a maid's outfit."

I nudged her playfully in the ribs. "Oi, cheeky."

"She may have a point. Aren't you going to introduce us?"

"Ryan, meet Diane, my lovely niece."

"Charmed, I'm sure." Ryan leaned over the bar, took Diane's hand and kissed it.

Diane smiled, clearly enjoying his attention.

"You're a true gent," I said, sarcastically.

"That's right. So, what can I get you lovely ladies?"

"Are you even open? It's just turned nine am."

"I'm stocking the shelves, but if I don't charge you it doesn't matter."

"Nothing for me, thanks. I've just come to pay my bill."

"I'll have a vodka and orange," Diane said.

"One orange coming right up." Ryan reached above the bar for a glass and then bent down to the fridge for a small bottle.

Diane nudged me, wiggled her eyebrows, and nodded at Ryan's nicely formed backside.

I shook my head and stifled a laugh.

He turned, poured the juice and handed it to Diane.

"You forgot the vodka," she said, cheekily.

"Sorry?" he said, cupping his ear. "I suffer from selective deafness." He winked at me. "Now, what can I get for you, pretty lady?"

"Oh, go on then. I'll have the same, thanks."

Ryan poured me a drink and then excused himself while he fetched my invoice.

"He fancies you," Diane hissed as soon as he was no longer in earshot.

"Give over." I laughed.

"He does!" she squealed. "Don't you fancy him?"

"No, I do not."

"Why not? He's hot."

I rolled my eyes shaking my head.

"What? He is," she said.

"I'm sure he is, but we're just friends."

"Yeah, but did you see how he looked at you?"

"He's a barman. That's what they do. He'll be like that with every woman who passes through this bar."

"Who will?" Ryan said, suddenly behind us.

Startled, I felt the blood rushing to my cheeks. "Oh, nothing." I eyeballed Diane, willing her to zip it.

"Here you go, then. I only charged you for the one night."

"Are you sure? I'd rather pay you for the rest of the week."

"Why? It's not as if we're fully booked."

"Well, if you're sure?" I emptied my glass and slid off the stool.

"Although, if you want to make it up to me..." he winced comically.

"Go on."

"You could always let me take you out to dinner. As a way of thanks, of course."

I nodded, rolling my eyes. "Oh, but of course."

"Does that mean yes?"

"No. It means let me think about it."

"I'll call you, then, shall I?"

Diane smirked at me as we left the building.

"Don't say a word," I hissed.

"What? I wasn't."

The next stop was the carpet store. Diane stayed in the car texting Andre.

I found a carpet that was close enough to the existing carpet sample Robert had provided. I approached a middle-aged salesman who was seated at the sales desk engrossed in a pile of paperwork. "Excuse me."

The salesman glanced up startled.

"I'm trying to match this carpet and I believe I've found one that's close enough." I handed him the carpet sample.

"Ah, yes." He removed his wire-rimmed glasses and wiped the lens on the sleeve of his jumper. "We should be able to match it quite easily. How much do you need?"

"I'm not sure. I'll need to arrange for somebody to measure up for me."

"All our technicians are fully booked for the next couple of weeks, I'm afraid. Is that alright?"

Two weeks? I screamed inside my head.

"Is that a problem, miss?"

"I was hoping to get someone out there much sooner than that.

You see, we can't go back inside the property until it's been re-carpeted."

"Ah, have you been flooded too? That rain yesterday caught us all out."

"No. Not a flooding—a murder."

His breath caught in his throat, and he erupted into a fit of coughing.

"Sorry," he said, when he regained control. "Are you talking about that awful business up at the Hewitt house?"

"Yeah. Did you know them?"

"I met Eddie a couple of times at the gym. A top bloke. I'm so sorry."

I nodded. "Steph was my sister. Diane, their daughter, wants to move back into the house, but how can I allow her to see it like that?"

"You leave it with me, love. I'll get my son in to cover the shop and I'll come over to measure up myself. Least I can do."

"Are you sure?" I offered him my most grateful smile. "That's so kind of you."

"Don't worry about it. Give me an hour or two to organise myself, and I'll meet you up at the house."

Back at the car, I could tell Diane had been crying.

She quickly dried her eyes and turned to face the window.

"Are you okay?" I bent forwards and patted her knee.

She nodded.

"Shall I take you back to Robert's? You don't need to come to the house with me if you're having a bad day."

"No. I want to come with you. I really don't want to be alone right now—it makes me think, and I don't want to think."

"I know what you mean, hon. But going to the house again might mess your head up even more."

"I'm fine."

I turned the Land Rover around and headed for the house.

"Why don't you call Andre? Maybe he wants to come over for a while."

"He's gone off fishing with his uncle."

I nodded. "Is that what's upset you?"

"I'm not upset about him. To be honest, I don't even know if I like him anymore."

I swung into the driveway and killed the engine before responding. "I thought you really liked him. That's what you said a couple of days ago."

"I just don't *feel* anything at the moment." She glanced up at the house welling up once again as she gulped down her grief.

"That's perfectly normal, sweetie. The trauma of losing your parents has shattered your world. You're bound to question everything."

"But I just feel so weak and helpless. I'm angry at Dad. Because of him, my last memory is a bad one. I screamed at him." She began to sob.

"It's okay."

"I wish…" She wiped her eyes with her hands. "I wish I could just tell him I'm sorry. That I didn't mean any of those things."

"Do you think he didn't know that? You're his daughter. It's common for teenagers to fight with their parents. Gee, you should've seen some of the fights your mum and I had with our parents."

"I know all that, but I just can't help feeling I let them down."

"Come here." I pulled her into my arms, and she sobbed into my shoulder. My heart broke with unshed tears of my own. "You're going to go through a range of emotions over the next few weeks and months—maybe even years. Anger, guilt, frustration. There's no one-size-fits-all, sweetie. We all grieve differently."

She nodded and pulled away to wipe her eyes again.

I looked in the glove box and found a couple of serviettes. "Here you go." I handed them to her. "Now, what do you want to do? The carpet guy is coming around soon, but we still have time for me to drop you off at Robert's or at a friend's for a couple of hours."

"No. I want to go inside. I want to feel close to them."

I squeezed her hand. "Okay. Come on then. I'm bursting for the loo."

CHAPTER 20

Icy rain met us as we left the vehicle. We ran up the steps and in through the front door.

The stench was still in the air, but it didn't seem quite as bad as yesterday.

With my hands clasped at my crotch, I ran into the downstairs bathroom, leaving Diane standing in the hall. "Sorry, sweetie, I won't be a tick," I called through the open door.

I heard her chuckling at the unladylike torrent of urine that hit the bowl.

"Stop laughing!" I cried, in mock disgust.

As I glanced around, my heart broke–I took in all the personal items that clearly belonged to my sister. A pair of diamante earrings on the windowsill, her makeup bag tucked tidily on a shelf, coconut water body wash in the shower. If we were going to be staying here, we'd need to go through everything and put all this type of stuff away until we were in the right mind to deal with it. But I'd prefer to do it alone—Diane wasn't strong enough.

The doorbell rang. I quickly washed my hands and rushed out of the bathroom just as Diane opened the front door.

"Oh, hi," I said to the man from the carpet shop who was

standing on the doorstep. "Diane, this is… Sorry, I didn't get your name."

"Nigel." He held his hand out towards her.

"Diane's my niece," I said. "That was quick, by the way."

"Yes, I rang a couple of the guys and told them the situation. They've agreed to come after work and install your carpet for you. I figured I'd best get the measurements and make sure we have enough on the roll."

"You don't know how relieved I am. Thanks so much."

I showed Nigel upstairs, and Diane followed close behind.

I was surprised how much Robert had done. The bedroom was empty, and all the furniture was stacked in the spare bedroom. The carpet and underlay were gone. He'd also removed the landing carpet and, thankfully, there was no sign of any blood.

"I'm going to my room," Diane said.

I nodded offering her a tight smile. Then I quickly rolled my eyes at Nigel once she was out of sight.

He patted my shoulder his eyes filled with pity.

Suddenly choked up, I left him to it and went back downstairs.

With Diane occupied, I found a plastic shopping bag in a kitchen drawer and headed back to the bathroom. I collected all the personal items I could and placed the bag in the garage. Then I had a quick sweep through the lounge and kitchen removing anything obvious.

Steph had OCD when it came to the housework, and everything had a place. So, unlike my house, there wasn't a lot of clutter lying around, thank goodness.

Nigel tapped on the kitchen door and pushed it open. "Okay, we have plenty of the carpet you chose to do that job. Christian and Mike will be here right after their last job, around five-thirty."

"I really appreciate this," I said. "I'm hoping to get Diane back into some kind of routine as soon as possible, but it's difficult when there's such a huge reminder of what went on right there on the stairs."

"Awful business." Nigel shook his head sadly. "Are the police any closer to catching who did it?"

"Not heard anything, so probably not. It doesn't appear to have been a robbery, or not that we can tell, anyway."

He shook his head. "You know, I was born in Carlisle sixty-three years ago," he said. "I've never wanted to move anywhere else until recently."

"Believe me, Carlisle isn't as rough as most other areas. Of course, there will be crime everywhere, but, on the whole, this place is relatively safe," I said.

"I put the world's problems down to drugs, you know. Young kids have no ambition. All they want to do is get high. But without a job where do they get the money to feed their habit? The poor buggers have no option but to go out and steal it."

I exhaled noisily. "I think you're being too generous. Most of them know what they're doing when they get on the drugs. Come on, you'd have to live on another planet not to have heard all the warnings."

"Yeah, you're right. Well, it's been lovely chatting with you, miss. I'll get off and leave you to it."

I saw him to the door and closed it behind him.

"I didn't think he was ever gonna go." Diane appeared at the top of the stairs.

"Aw, he's harmless. It's good of him to sort everything out for us the way he has, so the least I can do is humour him."

She trudged down the stairs and sat on the bottom step. "Did you see the way he looked at me?"

"What do you mean?" I said, thinking she meant he'd been sleazy.

"With those eyes—like a spaniel."

"He was just being sympathetic. He wants to help."

"I know. But I hate it. That's why I don't want to see my friends. I don't want them to look at me like that. Andre and his mum were doing it the other day."

"I know, but it'll pass."

"I hope so. Will we stay here tonight?"

"I don't think so. Once the carpet is fitted, we'd have to arrange to get the furniture taken out of the spare room. Maybe tomorrow."

"Andre could possibly help us tomorrow."

"Oh, is it all back on with you two?"

She grinned. "My head's all over the place."

"I know it is, sweetie. Right, we've got until five-ish. What do you want to do for the afternoon?"

Her face lit up.

"What is it?"

"Will you help dye my hair?"

I pulled her up from the step and into a bear hug. "I thought you'd never ask."

CHAPTER 21

We locked up and went back to Robert's via the chemist where Diane chose a rich, warm brown hair dye.

"Where should we do it?" I asked. "The last thing we want is to drip hair dye all over Robert's house. He'd kill us."

Her head snapped up, her eyebrows furrowed.

"That was an unfortunate turn of phrase, I'm sorry."

She grinned. "You're right though. He would go bonkers if we made a mess."

"I'm beginning to think we should go back to your house," I said.

"We can if you want?"

"I think it's for the best. Let's have some lunch first, and then we'll shoot back there."

I made us both a toasted cheese and onion sandwich, but Diane just picked at hers. She still looked a bit vague and spaced out after her earlier melt-down. I figured maybe the situation was only just hitting her.

The phone rang as we were leaving the house. I tentatively answered it.

"Could I speak to a Ms Carmichael, please," an oldish sounding gentleman said.

"Speaking."

"It's Reverend John speaking. Robert asked me to speak to you regarding your sister and brother-in-law's funerals."

"Ah, yes. Thanks for calling, Reverend."

"I wondered if it would be okay to call around to see you in the morning, or whenever is convenient, just to get an idea of the order of service."

"Yes, I'm sure that's fine. However, the police haven't released the bodies yet."

I heard a gasp behind me and I spun around to see Diane had wandered back inside.

I frantically tried to remember what I'd said out loud.

"Oh, okay. Well, it's up to you, of course. I can leave it until then if you like?"

"No, I don't suppose it matters. I was thinking of taking Diane away for a few days next week." I glanced at her, my eyebrows raised in question. "I guess it will be best if we have everything planned beforehand."

"Splendid. I shall come over first thing, then. Say ten am?"

I hung up and turned back to Diane. "I'm sorry about that, sweetie. That was Reverend John."

"Mum and Dad weren't even religious," she said, shaking her head.

"I don't suppose it matters—clearly Robert is, so, if you don't mind maybe we should go along with his arrangements."

She shrugged. "I guess."

"The reverend will be over at ten tomorrow morning, and then how do you fancy going to Manchester for a couple of days?"

"Don't mind," she said sadly.

"I think it might do you good to get away from here for a while. Give you a chance to come to terms with everything."

"But what about Andre?"

"What about him? He'll still be here when you get back."

"So we will be coming back?"

"Of course, we will. I'm just meaning for a few days, that's all."

"But you won't want to stop around here forever, will you?"

"Let's not even think about that for now. We've enough to contend with without making those kinds of decisions. Now come on. Let's go and dye your hair."

THE WIND HADN'T LET up all afternoon, but at least it had stopped raining by the time we got to the house.

We set up in the downstairs bathroom, taking in a stool from the breakfast bar, and I got to work.

"What made you want to dye it back to your natural colour?" I asked as I snapped on the pair of latex gloves provided.

Her eyes welled up. "It was all Mum could talk about. Every time I saw her she begged me to get rid of the *brassy peroxide*—her words. I got a bit of a kick out of it if I'm honest. Now I just wish I could do something that would make her proud of me."

"She was always proud of you, sweetie. She adored you."

"I wish I'd made her life a little easier. Uncle Rob was right. I was horrible to them sometimes."

"Well, I think it's a lovely thing to do in the memory of your mum. I'm sure she'll be dancing a jig at the thought of getting rid of that brassy peroxide." I grinned.

"Don't you like it either?

I shook my head. "Sorry, but no. I remember your natural curls were so beautiful. Whatever you've used to bleach it has dried it out like straw. It'll take more than a dye to sort it out, but at least that's a start."

The results were remarkable. Yes, as predicted, the ends of her now chocolate brown curls were still dry and porous and would need weeks of intense conditioning treatments before it would even resemble her original hair, but it looked a sight better than the blonde.

"So, what do you think?" I asked when she looked in the mirror for the first time.

A huge grin spread across her face. "I hate to admit it, but Mum was right."

I hugged her to me, certain that if there was an afterlife Steph would be giving me a high five at that moment.

"Right, we have an hour before the carpet guys will be here. Is there anything you want to do?"

"Would you mind if I popped across the road to see my friend Talia? I want to show off my new look."

"Not at all," I said with a smile, thrilled she seemed a little better than earlier.

"I can wait for the guys to arrive if you'd prefer not to be alone?"

"Don't be silly." My stomach was in knots. "I'll put my feet up and read my book for a while."

"Are you sure?"

I wanted to beg her to stay, but instead I nodded. "Certain," I said. My lie sounded genuine to my own ears.

"What time do you want me back by?"

"We'll need to arrange dinner, if you're hungry. Otherwise, just come back when you're ready. I'll be here."

I walked her to the front door and had to hold the handle tight to stop the wind flinging it open.

Diane's hair slapped about her face, then was plastered up against her pale cheeks. She pushed it back with both hands and raced off down the driveway.

CHAPTER 22

Diane had already turned the corner and was out of sight before I realised I hadn't asked which house her friend lived at.

The wind whistled through the trees and the branches bent and waved. I shuddered noticing the sky had turned a dark, moody grey. I suspected it would rain again soon.

I closed the door, pressed my back against it, and shuddered once again. I prayed the carpet guys wouldn't be too much longer.

In the lounge, I turned on a side light and sat on the cold leather sofa. Although I thought I was being strong for Diane, in truth she was keeping me sane. Being alone made me think about my own demons, and I wasn't in the right headspace yet.

I quickly got to my feet and went through to the kitchen. Finding a rubbish bag in the bottom drawer, I set about emptying the fridge. I poured a curdled bottle of milk down the sink before washing the bottle out. A brown package of sliced turkey smelled a little funky, so I threw it into the rubbish bag. A bowl of leftover meatballs made my heart ache. I imagined Steph had lovingly hand-rolled each one.

Most of the vegetables were fine, except for a half-eaten

cucumber that had turned to mushy green water inside the plastic sleeve.

I filled the sink with hot soapy water and began wiping clean all the surfaces. It didn't look dirty, quite the contrary, but I knew the forensic team would've pored over the entire place.

Once satisfied with the kitchen, I went through to Eddie's office. I tidied a few piles of paperwork into the desk drawers, not able to deal with anything yet but needing to move anything that might indicate the people who put them there would be right back. Once again, I noticed the broken door lock and made a mental note to get someone out to fix it.

After clearing the desk of papers and personal items, I ran a wet cloth over the top of it, and the filing cabinet. There'd be plenty of time to go through everything bit by bit once the funeral had been and gone.

Startled by the sharp peal of the bell, I rushed to answer the door.

The weather had taken a downturn and two men almost burst through the door in their bid to get out of the unseasonal icy rain.

"Hi, I'm Mike. This is Christian," the older of the two men said, holding his hand out.

I liked him immediately. Although I was so relieved simply to see another person, I'd have welcomed him with open arms even if he was an obnoxious jerk.

After a few more blustery moments, they carried the carpet and underlay inside and upstairs.

I hovered around a little, but it soon became apparent I was getting in the way, so I trudged back downstairs to read my book.

By six-thirty, the carpet was laid, and the men braved the squally weather as they ran to the van once again.

There was still no sign of Diane, which I thought was strange, but I didn't want to bother her after the week she'd had. I closed the lounge curtains, found the thermostat to switch on the heating, and returned to the sofa with my book.

Thump-thump-thump.

The loud bangs jolted me from my near doze. I felt a sickening feeling in my gut. "Who's there?" I called out, praying it was just Diane playing tricks on me.

Thump-thump-thump.

Prickles began to form on my entire body. I slid off the sofa, looking about for something to use for protection, but nothing presented itself as a weapon. Hugging myself, I shivered. Despite the heating, it was still really cold.

In the hallway again, I turned the thermostat dial up another couple of notches.

Thump-thump-thump.

The sound was coming from upstairs.

The wind howled around the house, and I once again thought about Diane. How stupid of me not to get the exact address. I still had a lot to learn about raising children.

With my arms crossed about my chest, I slowly climbed the stairs. My rational mind knew the wind was blowing something onto the side of the house, but my imagination was running riot.

Thump-thump-thump.

I jumped and squealed, bracing myself on the banister. The sound was much louder now and seemed to be coming from the master bedroom.

"Don't be such a pussy," I mumbled, and forced myself up the last few stairs.

I shuddered imagining Eddie's dead body as I skirted around the spot where he'd been found.

Another series of thumps caused my feet to leave the carpet.

Bracing myself, hand on the doorknob, I took a deep breath. Then I quickly rushed forward into the empty room.

All appeared normal. I couldn't find a thing that could've been making the sound. I peered from the window to the blustery weather beyond.

Thump-thump-thump.

Startled once again, I realised it was coming from the en suite bathroom.

I looked around the door of the miniature bathroom. A built-in shower cubicle, sink and toilet had been crammed into the tiny space. I noticed the toiletries in that room were for men which explained why Steph's stuff had been in the downstairs bathroom.

A movement above the toilet alerted me to the cause of the sound. The window had blown open and was swinging freely.

Relieved, I yanked it closed and pressed the stay firmly in place.

But, halfway down the stairs, another sound had the hackles up on my neck—a rattle, followed by a crash.

Feeling instantly sick, I began trembling uncontrollably and didn't know whether to run back upstairs or to face the cause of the sound head on.

My heartbeat thudded in my ears as I slowly descended the stairs. Reaching the kitchen, I gasped. The back door was wide open, and leaves and twigs had blown in all over the pristine kitchen floor.

I rushed forwards slamming it shut. The rattle, I realised, was the vertical blinds fitted to the door. Bending to gather the mess together, I spotted several wet footsteps.

My mind in a whirl, I slowly stood upright.

The sound of footsteps rooted my own feet to the tiles.

Diane suddenly appeared in the doorway rubbing her hair with a towel. "Oh, there you are," she said.

"What the…?" I shook my head. "I wondered who the hell had barged in here leaving the door wide open like that."

"Oh, sorry. I needed the toilet. I knocked on the front door and when you didn't answer I ran around the back. I thought I'd shut the door behind me, but I was in a bit of a rush."

"You frightened the life out of me," I continued, not yet ready to let it go.

"I said I'm sorry. I didn't think."

I shuddered and rolled my eyes at her. "I thought my time was up."

"You mean, you thought the killer was back?" Her eyes bulged.

"I did, I must admit."

"I'm sorry," she said again.

"It's okay. I'm glad it was only you though." I grinned, trying to lighten the mood. "You're late back. I was getting worried."

"I left my bag behind with my phone and my keys inside." She nodded to the shoulder bag hooked over the back of the stool at the breakfast bar. "But Talia's mum dropped me off. I was sure you'd see the headlights."

"I was upstairs. The bathroom window was banging in the wind."

"Oops. That explains it."

I shoved her arm playfully. "Come on. Let's get going. I'm starving."

CHAPTER 23

Back at Robert's, I set about making more cheese and onion toasties. "Not very nutritious," I said. "But I'll stuff you with vegetables tomorrow to make up for it."

Diane pretended to gag. "You know I hate veggies."

"All of them?"

"I don't mind potatoes if they're chips."

"Chips don't qualify as vegetables!"

"Why not? They come from potatoes and potatoes come from the ground—so why not?"

I shrugged. "I dunno. But they don't. Do you like carrots?"

She shook her head. "Too orange."

"Broccoli?"

"Too green."

"What are you actually on about? You can't dislike something because of the colour."

"*I* can."

"Then I suggest you learn to shut your eyes while you eat because vegetables will definitely be on the menu from today onwards."

She didn't reply.

I glanced up at her to see why.

Her tired eyes seemed to focus on something halfway up the wall. She chewed at her thumbnail.

"Penny for them."

She sniffed and shook her head as though trying to rid herself of a memory. "Mum tried everything to get me to eat vegetables."

"I'm sorry. I didn't mean to imply she didn't."

"I know you didn't. But I could've been talking to her just then. You remind me of her so much, which is good. Only sometimes it makes me sad."

I wiped my hands on a tea towel, walked over to her and wrapped her in my arms. "It will keep coming in waves. Grief is a strange thing. You can be laughing one minute and doubled up in physical pain the next."

"When will it stop?"

"Truth?"

She nodded.

"It won't ever completely go away. You'll learn to cope with it though. Well, most of the time, at least."

We ate in silence, each of us engrossed in our own thoughts. At bedtime, Diane hopped in beside me without discussion.

REVEREND JOHN TURNED out to be much younger than he sounded on the phone. He was in his late forties, clean shaven, with piercing blue eyes and glossy black hair parted to the side.

"I'm so sorry for your loss," he said to both Diane and me in turn, shaking our hands in earnest.

He declined a hot drink and got down to business almost right away.

"So what kind of service would you like?" he asked.

"Nothing religious," Diane blurted.

I eyeballed her and shook my head.

Reverend John smiled. "She's fine," he said to me before returning his gaze to Diane. "Were your parents not religious then, Diane?"

She shook her head. "I don't think so. They never went to church. Uncle Robert said he and Dad used to as kids."

"We don't have to have a Christian service, but are you okay about it being held at the church?"

She glanced at me before nodding. "I can deal with that."

"Okay. Now, Mister Hewitt suggested they were to have a joint service. Are you happy with that?"

Diane looked at me again.

I nodded. "I'd like that. Wouldn't you, Diane?"

She nodded too.

For the next hour, Reverend John dug and delved expertly extracting lots of information we hadn't even thought necessary. We laughed and we cried, and, once he'd gone, I felt totally wrung out.

"What time is Andre meeting us?" I asked Diane.

"Around twelve. I thought we'd be there by now."

"It's only just after eleven. I'll get changed and then we can shoot off." I didn't really relish moving into my sister's old house, but what choice did I have? Diane had set her heart on it.

ANDRE WAS LEANING against the stone garden wall as we pulled into the street.

"You're early," Diane said, grumpily, through the window.

I glanced at her as we drove through the gate onto the driveway. "That wasn't very nice. Are you not talking?"

She shrugged. "I'm still a bit miffed he went off fishing without telling me. He's supposed to be my boyfriend."

I indicated with my eyes that Andre had almost reached the car. She acknowledged it with a tiny nod of her head.

Andre seemed nervous, the way Diane and I had been when we first arrived at the house a couple of days ago. Thankfully, the stench had more or less vanished unless I was just getting used to it.

I was surprised at Diane's attitude towards her boyfriend. She hadn't shown me this side of her until now.

"Right. Should we get stuck in?" I said, taking over the situation. "We just need to move all the furniture from the spare room back into the master bedroom. It doesn't need to be in any order at this stage. I don't think either of us will want to sleep in there, will we?" I turned to Diane who shook her head. "Come on, then. The sooner we get it done the sooner we can move in."

Between the three of us, it didn't take long, although I did wonder how Robert had moved it all single-handedly in the first place. The heaviest items were the bed and a huge chest of drawers that were crammed full of clothes. The dressing table was filled with knick-knacks, which we placed into a box, along with books and any other smaller objects we came across. We stored the box in the wardrobe to deal with at a later date. Several times I felt as though I might have a panic attack. The familiar tightness in my chest alerted me it was on the cards. I forced myself to go through the breathing exercises I'd been shown after Giles had died.

Steph's perfume seemed to linger over every item, or maybe I'd just got it up my nose. Either way I found it overwhelming. I couldn't let Diane see how it was affecting me when she seemed to be coping so well.

Afterwards, we left the room, pulling the door closed. I felt the incredible weight lift from my shoulders.

CHAPTER 24

I left Diane and Andre sitting on her bed. Diane still appeared moody, and I thought they'd appreciate a little time alone.

"I'll go and pick up our bags and be right back," I said. "Should I grab something for lunch while I'm at it?"

"Yes, please." Andre nodded gratefully.

Diane shrugged.

I smiled and rolled my eyes. I couldn't remember being such a moody teenager, but I figured it was par for the course and I just needed to get used to it. "I'll go to the bakery and get us all a pie. Then we need to go food shopping later—I can feel my clothes stretching under the strain of all this fast food."

Silence.

Back at Robert's house, I was startled by a sound coming from the kitchen.

I crept across the hall and almost leapt from my skin as Cinnamon, the housekeeper, let out a piercing scream.

"Oh, Susanna, I didn't think anybody was home," she said, her hand clutching her throat dramatically.

"I'm sorry to startle you, Cinnamon. I just popped back for a few things, and then I'll be out of your hair."

I quickly went upstairs and grabbed the two holdalls Diane and I had packed before the reverend had arrived this morning. Taking a final glance around, I left. It wasn't the end of the world if we'd forgotten anything, seeing as Robert's house was through a small gate at the bottom of the garden—not that I'd ventured that far, yet.

I picked up a couple of filled rolls and three pies from the bakery and a carton of milk from the corner shop then headed back to the house. Each time I parked up outside the designer home, the feeling of doom seemed a little bit less than before.

My phone rang as I entered the house. I rushed to the kitchen and plonked the paper bags on the worktop. Then I rummaged in my bag for the phone.

Detective Conrad Jenkins flashed on the screen. I accepted the call.

"Hi, Detective. Long time, no speak. I was beginning to think you'd forgotten about us."

The Detective's gravelly chuckle made my ovaries clench, showing me my body at least hadn't given up on the hopes of ever having my own baby. "Not at all, Susanna. I apologise if you think I've been neglecting you?"

I grinned enjoying the playful banter. "I'll let you off. Now what can I do for you?"

He cleared his throat. "Just to confirm, there was no unknown DNA found at the crime scene."

"What does that mean?"

"Apart from Donald Macy, Eddie's business partner, we have no leads of enquiry. I was hoping Diane had remembered something else that might help us."

I shook my head and plonked down on the stool, feeling deflated. "No, nothing. All she remembers was the man wore a grey T-shirt and had a limp and a cough. I haven't come across anybody who resembles that description."

"That's what I was afraid of. Well, Donald Macy will be back in the country later in the week. Let's hope he can help us with our enquiries."

"Thanks, Detective."

"Conrad, please."

"Thanks, Conrad," I felt my cheeks flush.

"Oh, one last thing. It seems the killer did go into Diane's room looking for her. A drop of your sister's blood was on Diane's door."

"Do you think he intended to kill Diane too?"

A gasp from the hallway startled me. I looked up to see Diane standing there, her hands clamped over her mouth.

"It certainly seems that way," he said.

"I've got to go, Detective. Thanks for calling." I hung up before he had the chance to say anything else, and I rushed to Diane—pulling her into my arms. "I'm sorry, Diane. I didn't mean for you to hear that."

"What did he say?" she eventually asked.

"He said the killer went into your room. They found a drop of your mum's blood on your door. But they still haven't found any of his DNA, so they have no leads."

"So the killer's still out there and he might come back to finish me off?"

"I very much doubt it, sweetie. He didn't have a beef with you."

Andre padded down the stairs on bare feet.

"Anyway, grubs up." I tried to make my voice upbeat. "I bet you're starving, aren't you?"

Andre nodded, glancing at Diane, a worried expression on his face.

"Who's for tea? Coffee?"

They both stared at me as though I had two heads.

"What?" I asked.

"We're kids. We're not allowed tea or coffee," Diane said.

"Since when? I always drank tea. In fact, your grandmother used to put it in my bottle when I was a baby."

"Times have changed since then."

"Oh, I wondered why you never accepted a drink off me. Well, unless you know where we might find a stash of drinking chocolate or juice, we're stuck with tea, coffee or water."

"I might try a coffee. How about you, Andre?" Diane said.

He nodded, his mouth turned down at the corners like some tough guy from a gangster movie.

"I'll brew. You get the plates, sweetie," I said.

As we ate lunch, I realised the tension had lifted between the kids. Diane's grumpy expression was gone. They were even laughing and joking with each other when they headed back up to her room to unpack her bag and play some music.

I cleared away the plates and cups and then carried my bag up to the bright and airy spare room.

With my door shut, I could drop the façade of the past few days. I allowed the tears to flow. I wished Giles was here—he'd know what to do. I felt as though I was being dragged along with no real direction. This wasn't a recent thing. I'd felt the same since Giles died. I had no aim and no point to my life without him.

I awoke to the sound of soft tapping coming from the door. Startled, I sat bolt upright. I hadn't meant to fall asleep. "Yes?" My voice sounded croaky.

"Andre's mum's here to pick him up. Did you want to see her?" Diane said.

"I'll be there in a minute."

I forced myself off the bed and over to the mirror realising how tired I actually was. My eyes had dark circles and lines curving out from underneath them. I rubbed my face with my hands, trying to remove any last trace of sleep then I went downstairs.

CHAPTER 25

"I love your hair that colour," Teresa was saying to Diane as I entered the room.

"Andre doesn't. He said I look like everyone else now."

I gasped. "No, you don't. You look lovely."

Diane eyeballed Andre comically.

He shook his head. "I told her it's nice, but it isn't as striking as the blonde."

"She'd have ended up bald if she carried on bleaching it like that." I laughed.

"At least she would stand out from the crowd if she was bald." Andre ducked as Diane made as if to throttle him.

"Hi, Teresa," I said, giving her a quick hug.

"Terri, please. Only my mum and the law call me Teresa."

I laughed. Something about this woman cheered me up. "Want a cuppa?"

"Love one, please. Coffee, no sugar."

"We might as well go back upstairs then," Diane said, sloping off and dragging Andre with her.

"So, how's everything?" Terri asked once we were alone.

I shrugged. "Okay, I guess. We seem to be coping."

"I was surprised you wanted to move back in here. I hope you don't mind me saying that."

"No. Not at all. And I felt the same, but this is Diane's home, and, despite what happened, she wants to be here."

"Yeah. I guess it's difficult. Poor love. I think she's doing remarkably well. Better than I'd be, to be honest."

"She has her wobbles. It's not always happy and jolly."

"No, I know that. But on the whole?"

"On the whole, she's doing amazingly well."

"And how do you feel?"

The way her eyes bored into mine suddenly unlocked the floodgates and tears soaked my cheeks.

She slid off her stool and rushed to my side, hugging me with a strength she didn't look capable of. "Let it out, girl. You'll feel much better for it."

I didn't need telling twice, and I sobbed like a baby, allowing her to comfort me. Normally I was doing all the comforting. Once my tears had dried, I felt a bit silly. "I'm sorry about that."

"Don't be sorry. You obviously needed to get it out. Do you feel any better?"

"Much. Thank you."

"Now, you sit yourself down and I'll finish the coffee," she said.

I didn't argue, glad of all the support I could get.

"Have you been sleeping?" Terri asked, placing two steaming mugs down on the breakfast bar.

"A little. But I've never been a great sleeper."

"Maybe not, but you do need to take care of yourself you know. Where would Diane be if you had a meltdown?"

I shuddered. How did she know I suffered from anxiety? Was it that obvious? "I know. To be honest with you, I wasn't in the best frame of mind before all this happened."

"Do you want to talk about it?"

I shook my head, but my traitorous mouth began blabbing anyway. "My husband died. It was almost four months ago.

Totally unexpected, no long illness or anything, and I very nearly had a nervous breakdown. I went away to our villa in Spain to try to get my head together. I love it there, and I didn't feel as though I was ready to come back anytime soon."

"And then this happened."

I nodded not wanting to go into too much detail about the real reason I came back. "I knew Diane would need me, so I packed up and was on the plane before I had a chance to think about the ramifications."

"How did your husband die? Don't answer if you don't want to tell me."

My breath caught in my throat. Should I tell her? Could I tell her? I'd only told Angel the details of what had happened. But Angel was a dear friend, and I didn't know this woman from a bar of soap. Yet something about her told me she was indeed a friend. I glanced at her unsure whether to trust my gut or to close down. "It's a long story."

"I don't have to be anywhere."

"Giles was my rock," I said. "I met him when I was twenty-years-old. He was a lot older than me—almost twice my age." I glanced up to see her reaction. Her expression didn't change.

"Nice. I've always been into older men." She smiled.

"My parents didn't trust him. They said he was out for a good time and it would never amount to anything. Steph also thought it would end in tears, but we loved each other. We got married a year later. I had the wedding of my dreams. Giles was well off. He was a property developer, and his company dealt in huge refits both here and in the States. He offered me a fabulous lifestyle."

"So what happened?"

"Giles withdrew into himself this past year. I didn't have a clue what was wrong. He refused to see a doctor insisting he was just stressed and tired and that it would all come right. One more deal here, one more refit there. It wasn't as though we needed the money, or so I thought." I paused, thinking back to the last few months of his life. Once I discovered what was wrong, of course, it was glaringly obvious. But it hadn't been at the time.

I got to my feet and walked over to the window, looking out at the dismal afternoon.

Terri cleared her throat and I turned around, suddenly remembering she was there.

"I'd gone to have a manicure, and when I got back I was surprised to see his Land Rover parked in his allocated spot. He'd been in New York for over a week, you see. I usually travelled everywhere with him, but he'd insisted that last trip he'd do alone. Said I'd distract him. I almost ran up the fifteen flights of stairs—the lift took so long to arrive. I couldn't wait to get inside. I'd missed him so much." My chest compressed as I thought back to that day. The memory played back as though in slow motion.

Terri got to her feet and guided me back to the stool. Then she rummaged through the cupboards for a glass and returned with some water. "Here, get this down you. You've gone so pale."

I gulped at the ice cold water greedily, suddenly parched, then I placed the glass down.

"When I got to our apartment—a duplex penthouse, the first he'd developed since we'd been together—I couldn't find him. I ran from room to room calling him."

I stopped willing myself to go on. To say the words. The tears were flowing again, but I didn't even try to wipe them away.

"I found him hanging from the rafters in the sun room. Giles had killed himself."

CHAPTER 26

"How bloody awful," Terri said, running a hand over my shoulders. "Why? What reason did he have to kill himself?"

"That's what's so utterly laughable." I rubbed at my temples, exhausted from all the tears. "Money. He hadn't paid his tax in the States and they were onto him."

"And you didn't know?"

I shook my head. "I didn't have the slightest inkling his troubles were financial. I suspected illness, or another woman. I even thought he'd stopped loving me."

"How much did he owe?"

I huffed out a sad laugh. "A lot. But not enough to kill yourself over, in my opinion. We may have had to lose our home and the villa, but we could've started again. At least we'd have had each other."

"I hope you don't think I'm being nosy, but how did you get to keep your home and the villa?"

"Because he'd put them in my name years ago. He'd also paid me a weekly wage since we met, kept it in a separate account in my name. It was as though he knew all along how it would end up. As if I would want the money and property without him. So now, although the business is gone, I have enough money from the nest egg and the insurance money to keep me afloat. I'll never need to get a job. The apartment and the villa were paid for so, in his eyes, I was set for life."

"I'm so sorry, Susanna. What a terrible shock it must've been to find him like that."

"It was. I just don't understand why he had to wait until he came home to do it. He had to know it would screw me up for life finding him like that."

"He obviously wasn't in his right mind. I mean, how difficult is it to plan your own death? He probably didn't even think about what would happen if he actually pulled it off. But in your home…?"

"Yeah." I sighed.

"Fancy a glass of wine?" Terri asked.

"I don't know if…" I shrugged.

"I have a couple of bottles in the car. That's if you've nothing better to do?"

"Best offer I've had in months," I said.

I found Steph's crystal wine glasses while Terri rushed out to the car for the wine. I glanced at the clock, almost 5pm and still no grocery shopping done.

"Fancy staying for dinner?" I asked as she returned with a bottle in each hand. "We could order a couple of pizzas?"

"Sounds fine to me. And I can't see us getting any complaints from the kids."

"I'll have to get Diane to order it. I wouldn't have a clue what's what."

I called up to Diane, and she took control.

We had a lovely evening. Almost normal, in a way. We were all relaxed and in good spirits. By the time they left I was exhausted, but content.

Diane helped clear the table, and we loaded the dishwasher between us. Then we sat in front of the TV for a couple of hours watching some mind-numbing reality show that Diane loved and I couldn't make head nor tail of.

At bedtime we trudged up the stairs together.

Diane used the bathroom first. I was shocked when she came out dressed in her pjs and hugged me goodnight before heading into her own room.

I'd automatically presumed she'd spend the night in my bed like she had every night since I'd arrived. I stood there staring at her closed door for an unnatural amount of time before heading into the bathroom myself.

Checking out my reflection in the mirror above the sink, I noticed, once again, my tired and haggard appearance. Even my hair, that used to be my pride and joy, looked dry and unkempt. I decided to take Diane for a much-needed spa day when we finally got to Manchester.

In the spare room, which was now my bedroom for the foreseeable, I closed the curtains and slid under the duvet of the king-sized bed.

I tossed and turned. Although exhausted, I couldn't seem to switch off my chattering brain. An unusual high-pitched sound startled me. I shot upright listening. Nothing. I snuggled back down. Maybe it had been a fox or a stray cat.

I couldn't sleep. A short time later, I got out of bed and opened the door. I felt so shut off from everything. A strange house, a strange room, a strange bed. I'd actually thought Diane would mooch into my room after a short while, but she didn't. It was embarrassing to admit she seemed to be coping better than me.

I climbed back into bed and stared at the ceiling. It was subtly glowing from the light of the pink salt-lamp on the side table.

BEING BACK *in the house seemed strange, so soon after the murders.*

I punched in the alarm code and exhaled in relief when silence continued.

After sweeping through the lounge and kitchen, I crept upstairs, taking my time and carefully avoiding the two creaky steps. Trying not to make a sound as I dragged my duff leg along the landing, I paused outside Diane's room. I pushed open her door, grinning once again at the Princess Di plaque.

THE FIRST PIERCING scream fused me to the mattress—my mind in a turmoil. I sprang to my feet and raced to Diane's room.

I found her at the far side of the room, crushed into the corner. "What happened? It's okay. I'm here, sweetie."

"He was here. I heard him."

"No. The alarm's set. There's nobody here. I promise you. It was just a dream."

She sobbed uncontrollably, gripping me to her with trembling arms. "He was here. Honestly, Aunt Susie. You've got to believe me."

I sat beside her on the carpet until her sobs subsided.

"Do you believe me?" she asked.

"Of course, I believe you. But I still think you may have been dreaming. We set the alarm."

"I heard him. He was in my room. You've got to believe me."

"I'll go and check downstairs. Wait here."

"No!" she cried. "Don't leave me."

"Come with me, then. We'll check the doors and windows, then you can get in bed with me, okay?"

She nodded.

Hand in hand, we walked down the stairs.

I felt a little sick as I walked across the landing and over the place where Eddie had been killed. I couldn't show Diane how freaked out it made me.

As we reached the bottom of the stairs, Diane gasped.

"What?"

"The alarm! It's been disarmed," she squealed. "See? I told you. He was here."

I could barely breathe. My world started to spin, but Diane needed me, and I needed to pull myself together.

We slowly crept from room to room holding onto each other for dear life. But there was no sign of any intruder and the doors and windows were all shut tight. Once we were certain we were alone, we sat in the kitchen. I heated two cups of milk in the microwave.

"So? Do you believe me?"

I rubbed my face and chewed at my bottom lip as I thought about the question. I wanted to reassure her—tell her there was no way it could've been the killer, but she'd seemed so certain. And somebody *had* turned off the alarm, or maybe I'd not set the thing correctly in the first place. I contemplated calling the police but decided against it. Nothing had been touched, and I hadn't seen anything. I could just imagine what Conrad would say to us for dragging him out of bed in the middle of the night because of a dream.

"Maybe I didn't set the alarm properly, sweetie. You know I'm a technophobe. And the doors are all secure. Who else has a key?"

"Just Uncle Rob."

"So, aside from us three, nobody has a key?"

She shook her head.

"And what about the alarm code?"

"Same. As far as I know. Just Uncle Rob."

"I'll call the security firm tomorrow and see if they can install a panic button as well as change the alarm code. Will that make you feel a little safer?"

She nodded. "I think so. I want to be here, but I can't bear the thought of him coming back for me."

"I won't allow that. Now, how about we take these upstairs and try to get some shut-eye?" I handed her a mug. "And then tomorrow, do you fancy a trip to Manchester for a few days?"

Her eyes lit up. "I'd love that."

"Come on, then. It'll be time to get up if we don't get our skates on."

I jammed a chair behind the door, to give Diane peace of mind.

We drank our milk and Diane snuggled beside me in the bed. She was snoring softly within a few minutes.

I felt my eyelids growing heavy the crushing exhaustion no longer held back by adrenaline or my frantic thoughts. I managed to get a few hours uninterrupted sleep.

THE SUN POURED in the room through a gap in the curtains. I lifted myself up onto my elbow. Diane was still sparked out and drooling on her pillow. Her nose twitched. I envied her ability to sleep so soundly.

I slid out of bed and removed the chair I'd wedged against the door. Then I trudged across the landing to the bathroom.

The shower spat cold water at me. I squealed, leaping backwards while fiddling with the dial. A steady stream of hot water finally washed over me and filled the bathroom with steam. I scrubbed my skin with a loofah then dumped a load of conditioner on my hair, needing to make more of an effort with my appearance.

Feeling a bit more refreshed, I dried myself off on a towel and brushed my teeth. I poked at the bags under my eyes and decided to disguise them with a dab of concealer and a layer of my old faithful, no-nonsense, foundation. I finished the look with a swipe of fuchsia pink lippy and waved the mascara wand over my lashes. Pleased I looked a little more human I went in search of my niece

"You smell nice," she said, still cosy in my bed. She shaded her eyes from the early morning sunlight.

"Thanks. More than I can say about you," I giggled.

She rewarded me with a pillow to the back of my head.

"Oi! Cheeky. Now go and get yourself prettied up if we're going to Manchester."

CHAPTER 27

DIANE RUSHED TO THE BATHROOM WHILE I HEADED DOWNSTAIRS. I was keen to check once more if I could see any sign of tampering on any of the doors or windows—there was nothing. However, the alarm was still set which was something, at least.

I found a few slices of bread in the freezer and shoved them in the toaster.

Diane came downstairs as I scraped the toast with plum jam.

"Fancy a cuppa?" I asked, sipping my tea.

She screwed her nose up. "I'll pass, thanks."

"Then get some of this toast down you. We won't be eating until we get to Manchester. I'll take you to my favourite restaurant in Chinatown."

She picked up half a slice of toast and began tappety-tapping away on her phone.

After breakfast, we each packed a bag before locking up the house. I made a mental note to get the alarm sorted while we were away. Then we loaded up the Land Rover and headed out of town.

"Do you think we should tell Detective Jenkins about last night?" Diane asked as we approached the motorway.

"I will if you want, but he may think it's odd we have no evidence, apart from the alarm being turned off."

"You think he'll think I'm crazy?"

I glanced at her disapprovingly. "I never said that. I just think it might confuse the investigation, and it's not as if we have anything to show him. But, like I said, I will if you want me to."

My phone rang, and went through to the hands-free kit.

I pressed the accept button. "Hello?"

"It's Robert. Where are you?"

His attitude got my back up right away. "On our way to Manchester. Why?"

"Because I got home last night to an empty house. I didn't think you meant to move out right away."

"We got the carpets replaced so there wasn't much point hanging around. And now we're going to stay in my apartment for a day or two."

"When were you going to tell me?"

"I didn't know I had to ask your permission, Robert. I am a grown woman."

He growled. "I didn't say you weren't. But it's common courtesy to let me know where you're taking my niece."

"*Our* niece. And last I heard you were gallivanting off around bloody Ireland." I glanced at Diane, conscious we shouldn't be sniping in front of her, but he knew how to push my buttons.

"I was visiting my elderly parents who, in case I need to remind you again, have just lost their eldest son."

Low blow. Now he made me look like a right bitch. "I do know that, Robert. And just for the record, what time did you get home?"

"Around midnight."

"So how did you know we'd left already?"

"I didn't. Not until this morning."

I smirked and winked at Diane. "That's not what you said

earlier. You said you got home to an empty house last night. Did you go snooping in our rooms again?"

"Don't be stupid. I meant I got home last night, but I didn't know you'd gone until this morning."

"So you didn't come over to the house last night and let yourself in?"

"What house?"

"Steph's house. Diane's house. You know which house I'm talking about. Did you, or didn't you?"

"Oh, I'm not even going to talk to you while you're like this."

"Just tell me. Did you let yourself into the house last night and turn off the alarm?"

"No. I. Did. Not. Now you tell me. How long do you intend staying away?"

"I'm not sure. I'll be in touch." I ended the call and glanced at Diane. "Sorry about that, sweetie."

"Do you really think he was the one who came in last night?"

"He was angry we had left his house. Maybe he was just concerned for us, sweetie."

"He does have a key. And he knows the alarm code. But what about the cough and the limp? I heard them again last night. Uncle Robert doesn't limp."

I gripped the steering wheel and exhaled noisily. "I really don't know, sweetie."

A COUPLE OF HOURS LATER, after picking up a bag of essentials from the supermarket, we drove into the underground carpark below the apartment block.

"Did your husband build this?" she asked. "It's massive."

"No. The building was already here. It used to be an office block."

"Oh. So what did he do?"

I parked the Land Rover in Giles' allocated spot and smiled at her. "He gutted it and redeveloped the building into twenty high-spec apartments."

"Did you keep the best for yourself?"

I chuckled. "What do you think?"

"I can't wait to see it." She grabbed her bag and was practically bouncing to get up to the apartment.

The usual feeling of dread I'd come to associate with my once beloved apartment was suddenly overshadowed by Diane's excitement, and I welcomed her positive energy.

When we took the lift up to the penthouse suite she squealed with delight. I couldn't help laughing along with her. The way she ran through the apartment brought tears to my eyes. She reminded me of the way I'd been when Giles showed me around for the first time.

"Is this my room?" she asked, running into the spare bedroom across the hall from mine.

"You can take your pick. There are two spare bedrooms. This one is closest to mine."

"Where's the other?"

"Upstairs. There's another large living room, two bedrooms and a sun room up there."

"Can I go and see?"

"Feel free. But please don't go into the room at the end of the hall." I couldn't remember if I'd locked it before I'd left.

Her eyebrows furrowed. "Aren't you coming up?"

"No. I'll leave you to it while I use the loo and unpack my bag. Then we can get ready to do a bit of sightseeing if you like?"

I laughed as she whooped all the way up the stairs.

Ten minutes later, we were in my BMW heading into town.

"Aunt Susie?" Diane said, thoughtfully.

"Yes."

"What's in the room at the end of the hall?"

I suddenly went cold. Trying to keep a lightness to my voice, I smiled. "It's filled with all sorts. Nothing for you to worry about. Did you choose which room you liked best?"

She nodded. "I preferred the upstairs one, but I'd rather be closer to you. It just seemed isolated up there on my own."

"To be honest, since Giles, I rarely go up there. I have everything I need downstairs."

"It is big. When you said you lived in an apartment, I imagined a poky flat. This is as big as our house, easily."

"Yeah. I probably don't need such a big place anymore."

She gasped. "So, will you sell it?"

"Who knows what the future will hold, sweetie? It's not all about me anymore—there are two of us to consider now, and I guess we need to decide where we want to live in the long run."

She nodded, suddenly a little morose.

"Anyway, less of that. I hope you're starving. I'm going to take you to *the* best Chinese restaurant in the western world."

"How do you know I even like Chinese?"

I did a double-take and clocked her grin. "Ah, you had me then." I laughed.

I pulled into my usual carpark just outside Chinatown. "Come on, we need to walk. One thing you'll learn about the city is you can't find any parking where you need it."

She didn't mind. She was all wide-eyed and giddy.

CHAPTER 28

"Haven't you been to Manchester before?" I asked, surprised, as I steered her down the back streets to Chinatown.

"No. I went with my dad to London once. I stayed in the hotel watching movies while he went to his meetings, and then he took me to the cinema and for a burger afterwards."

"Didn't he show you any of the sights? London is a fantastic city."

"No. It was a waste of time, really. But I didn't complain. It was nice to spend time just the two of us."

"So you weren't always at loggerheads?"

"No, not back then. I was his princess."

I smiled sadly and wrapped my arm around her shoulders as we trudged along the brightly decorated, busy street.

"Here we are." I nodded at the gaudy, gold-painted entrance of my favourite restaurant. I hadn't been since well before Giles died, but I figured life goes on. For all the heartache Steph and Eddie's death had caused, it had also given me a reason to live.

"Are we going in then, or what?" Diane laughed.

I smiled and led her up the grand staircase, blinking back tears. In my mind's eye, I saw the hundreds of times Giles whisked me up and down those stairs over the years. Maybe this hadn't been a good idea after all. But as I looked down at Diane's twinkling eyes, I sighed and forced a smile. "You're in for a treat."

Once we'd eaten our weight in prawn crackers, spring rolls, chicken chow mein and crispy duck, we hobbled back down the stairs, too full to feel good.

"What do you want to do now?" I asked.

"My stomach hurts," she groaned.

I laughed. "Tell me about it. But we can't waste the rest of the afternoon."

"What choices do we have?"

"Manchester Museum? It's years since I've been around there."

"No thanks. Why would I want to traipse around a load of old stuff?"

"Diane! Wash your mouth out. That's history, and it's bloody interesting."

"For you, maybe. Not me."

I rolled my eyes. "Come on then. What do you want to do?"

"Piccadilly Gardens sounds fun. Mum told me she used to meet Dad in Piccadilly. He used to get the train down from Carlisle when they were first going out."

"Oh, that's not far. Come on. It'll do us good to walk our meal off."

Piccadilly Gardens was buzzing. Although it wasn't a sunny day, it was the end of the school holidays, and it appeared everyone must've had the same idea.

Diane was in awe. It did my heart good to watch her delight at the simplest things.

"Can we go on a tram one day?"

I nodded. "If you like." I spied an elderly couple preparing to leave, and I stopped beside their bench.

"We're going now, love," the kindly faced woman said, patting the bench beside her.

I smiled and nodded.

We quickly sat down as soon as they stood up.

"You have to be fast around here," the man chuckled.

"You're not wrong," I said.

We spent the best part of an hour people watching, something Steph and I used to do as kids. I'd forgotten how enjoyable it could be, especially in a city that was as culturally diverse as Manchester.

Afterwards, we strolled back to the car.

"I wish I'd got to come here with Mum," Diane said, as she linked her arm in mine.

"Me too."

"She often spoke about you."

"Really?"

"Yeah. She said you were always jetting off somewhere or other. That you didn't have time for us."

"That's not true. I would've always made time for you if you'd said. I just got caught up in my own life. That's all."

We reached the car, and I realised Diane had withdrawn into herself again.

"What's on your mind?" I asked, as I put the key in the ignition.

"Oh, you know. Just stuff."

"Stuff meaning your mum?"

She breathed in slowly through her nostrils. "I'm sorry to spoil the day. It's just that I know she'd have loved this. I miss her so much."

"I know you do, sweetie. Me too." I hugged her and stroked her hair until I felt her energy shift. "You okay now?"

She nodded. "I'm just a bit worried that having me will cramp your style."

I turned on the engine. "Cramp my style? I wasn't aware I even had a style to cramp, especially not nowadays."

"It's a lot to take on though. I get that."

"You have no idea how lonely I've been lately. You, my dear, are like a breath of fresh air. We can help each other through the dark moments."

"What about when you meet a new boyfriend? You won't want me playing gooseberry."

"I don't know if I'll ever want a new boyfriend. But if I do, I'd make it clear that we come as a package deal."

"But what if you want babies of your own?"

"I won't. I wasn't as lucky as your mum. She got pregnant right away and never looked back."

"She thought you were jealous of her, you know. Because she had me, and you couldn't get pregnant."

"I was a little jealous when I first discovered she was having twins." I gasped, realising I might have slipped up.

"It's okay. I know I had a baby brother. Mum puts a new rose bush in the garden every year on our birthday, which, of course, was the day of his death."

"At first I felt guilty. I'd been complaining to Giles how unfair it was. I couldn't have one baby, and she was having two just like that." I clicked my fingers. "You can imagine how terrible I felt when I discovered your brother was stillborn."

"It wasn't your fault. He hadn't developed properly, and, because of the way we lay, the scan hadn't picked up on it."

"After that, my own babies died one by one, and I stupidly blamed myself. If I hadn't cursed Steph with my spiteful thoughts, then her baby would've lived and so would mine."

"Did you really think that?"

"At my lowest moments, yes."

She placed her hand on my knee, and I squeezed it with my own. "It wasn't your fault, and it wasn't mine."

"Of course it wasn't yours," I said. "How could it be?"

She shrugged. "My dad always said the wrong twin died."

"What?" I gasped and grabbed hold of her hand. "That's bullshit! Your dad had no right saying that. It's downright nasty." I was seething. How could anybody say something like that to their own child?

WHEN WE ARRIVED HOME, I walked up the stairs and indicated for Diane to follow me.

"What for?"

"You know when you asked me what was in the other room earlier?"

She nodded, wide-eyed.

"I wasn't entirely honest with you." I unlocked the door and allowed it to swing inwards.

The room was the saddest place on earth for me. Four identical white swinging cribs stood along the back wall. The room was filled with pinks and lemons and blues. Teddy bears hung from a huge mesh hammock in the back corner. Four picture frames, each displaying one teeny handprint and one teeny footprint, were on the wall behind the cribs, the first in pink the rest in blue.

Diane gasped when she glanced inside the cribs.

"Don't worry. They're not real." I plucked one of the lifelike handmade dolls out of the crib. "This is Jack. I'm not crazy. It's just something I had to do after they died."

"Is this what you would call a shrine?"

I nodded. "I guess it is. But I couldn't just allow them to be forgotten. They were my babies. Not one or two miscarriages. Four living, breathing children. My children."

"They're so real."

"Giles had them made for me. He took hundreds of photos so they're identical in features, size and weight as my babies had been at birth."

"That's so sad," she whispered, stroking Jack's face.

"Hold him, if you like. He was your cousin after all."

She hesitated at first and then held her arms out to take him from me.

"He's the reason I rushed back from Spain—it was his birthday and also the anniversary of his death, and I almost missed it. So, when you asked if I could sell this place, the answer is probably not. Even though I don't need to sit in here every day, caring for and loving these babies all the time, the thought of parting with them tears my heart in two. I know they're not my babies. They're just exquisitely moulded plastic, but it's what they represent. So, even if I don't ever come in here again, my babies will all lie together in here. And if that makes me crazy then so be it."

Diane's eyes had misted over. "I don't think it's crazy. I think it's lovely."

"Unhealthy is what most people would say, but it got me through an awful time, and I'm grateful."

She handed Jack back to me and stroked the cheeks of each of the other babies in turn.

I placed the baby back into his crib and covered him up lovingly. "So now you know my deepest, darkest secret do you still want to live with me?"

"I'd be honoured to live with you, Aunt Susie. I think you're amazing."

CHAPTER 29

I slept like a log for the first time in ages. Diane initially got in her own bed, but I felt her slide in beside me sometime in the middle of the night.

"You okay?" I murmured, my eyes still shut tight.

"Yes."

The next morning, we were both well rested and more chilled out than we'd been all week.

"Do you fancy going for a pamper day at a spa?"

Her eyes boggled, and she grinned. "You mean like a manicure?"

"Manicure, pedicure, facial. They even have a hair salon there if you want a trim and deep conditioning treatment."

She squealed and hugged my neck. "I can't wait to tell Talia. She'll have kittens."

"I can't promise anything, but I'll give them a call now. If not today, we'll hopefully be able to get in before we go back to Cumbria."

I rang the spa and was relieved to hear a familiar voice on the other end of the phone. "Gill, how the bloody hell are you?" I said in my best telephone voice.

"Well, Susanne Carmichael if I live and breathe. Where the heck have you been?"

"Long story, babe. But I have my lovely niece with me for a couple of days. You couldn't book us in for the works, could you? Then maybe I can catch you up over a drink at the bar."

"Today?"

"If you can."

"Er, yeah. We should be able to do that. There may be a little wait in between procedures, but you can go for a swim or a sauna."

"Sounds great. I'll see you soon."

We breakfasted on toast and jam before heading across the city.

Driving into the impressive property, I parked the BMW outside the entrance to the flash glass building.

We spent the entire day being prodded, poked, and manipulated within an inch of our lives. Then we met up at lunchtime, dressed in fluffy white robes and turbans.

After eating a chicken salad each, we went our separate ways again.

I finished before Diane and, as promised, met up with Gill for a natter. My eyes almost popped out of my head when Diane came through. Her hair had been styled and straightened. She looked gorgeous.

"How was it?"

"Okay." She eyed Gill warily, and I recognised her expression as one of annoyance.

I drained my glass and got to my feet. "It was lovely to catch up with you, Gill. But I'd best get this pretty young lady home. It's been a long day."

I waited until we were in the car before I asked her what was wrong.

"That was pure torture."

"What was?"

"She picked at my skin with a hook! It was agony. She cut one of my cuticles and made it bleed."

I gasped and looked at her hands.

She pointed out the finger that did indeed have a crescent shape cut into her skin below the nail.

"Oh, my God. Did you move?"

"No, I didn't move. Stupid bitch didn't even care I was gushing blood. Then another evil bitch almost broke my back. Why do people put themselves through something so horrible?"

I rubbed my mouth, trying my best to stop myself from laughing. "Was there anything you did like?"

"My hair's cool. That's about it. I know it probably cost you a fortune to do that for me, but do me a favour in future and don't bother. I hated every minute of it."

"Well, if it's any consolation, you look amazing."

"Do I?"

"Take a selfie and send it to Andre. I guarantee he won't say you look like every other girl now."

The corners of her mouth twitched. "You look pretty hot too."

"Why, thank you, ma'am. Where should we go to show it off?"

"I wouldn't mind getting something to eat that isn't rabbit food."

I grinned. "I did notice you left most of your salad. Fancy a burger?"

She grinned, chewing her lip excitedly.

I took her to the Handmade Burger Co. on Deansgate—somewhere I'd heard was popular with all the youngsters. I wasn't very adventurous when it came to burgers, so I ordered the classic with chips.

Diane, practically salivating, ordered a peanut butter and bacon burger with onion rings.

I couldn't believe the size of the burgers when they arrived. Mine, although smaller than Diane's, was almost as big as my head.

We had a good go at devouring them, but, in reality, we would've still had some left over if we'd shared one between us.

Afterwards, we walked the food off and ended up in the cinema watching an American comedy.

Walking back to the car a couple of hours later, I turned on my phone. The familiar tone told me I'd received a voice message.

"The police have released the bodies for burial," Robert's voice boomed. "Call me. We need to arrange a date for the funerals."

I glanced at Diane as I hung up.

"What?" she asked.

"That was Robert. They've released your parents' bodies."

"Do we have to go home?"

"Not right away. It's Friday tomorrow and then the weekend, so we won't be able to organise anything until next week at the earliest." I reached for her hand. "You okay?"

She smiled and shrugged. "I guess. You?"

"I'll be better when I get these shoes off. I'm ready for home now. Are you?"

"Lightweight." She grinned cheekily.

We had a lovely weekend. The fact we were away from Cumbria enabled Diane to put everything to the back of her mind, and she only had a couple of wobbles here and there. On Saturday, we took a trip around the city on the tram, then we strolled past the Manchester Arena, the shocking scene of the bombing. Diane was a huge fan of Ariana Grande and it meant a great deal to her.

Early Monday morning, we loaded up the car and set off back to Carlisle.

"How did Uncle Giles die?" Diane suddenly blurted out as we drove on to the motorway.

I gripped the steering wheel and exhaled slowly.

"I'm sorry. Don't tell me if you'd rather not."

I shook my head and poked a finger in the corner of my eye. "It's okay. I promised I'd tell you. It's just really difficult."

She faced the road directly ahead.

"Giles had a lot on his plate. His businesses were struggling in the States, but he didn't tell me about it. If he had, then maybe we could've dealt with it together." I indicated and pulled over onto the hard-shoulder to grab a pack of tissues from the glove box.

"I'm sorry. I shouldn't have brought it up."

I struggled to swallow. Then I decided instead of trying to stop the tears to let them flow. I sobbed into the tissue. After a few minutes, I managed to pull myself together enough to speak again. "Giles killed himself."

"No!" she cried. "Why would he do that?"

"Money. He faced bankruptcy or death—he chose death."

"That's terrible."

I wiped my eyes in the rear-view mirror. "Please keep it to yourself. There's such a stigma associated with suicide."

"I won't tell a soul, I swear." Diane was gripping my knee. "So what happened with the company in the end?"

"Everything was sold to pay the debts. He left me enough to live on quite comfortably, and, of course, I have the two properties."

"But couldn't both of you have lived on the same amount?" Diane asked me.

I laughed sadly. "You'd think so, right? It must've been a male pride thing. That's all I can put it down to."

"I just don't get it."

"Me neither. That's what made it so difficult to deal with. It's not as if I'm money mad. We could've managed quite comfortably." I put the gear stick in drive and indicated into the traffic. I felt surprisingly relieved we had no more secrets between us.

CHAPTER 30

I stepped inside the hallway and froze as I realised the house alarm had been disarmed, again. The hairs on my neck stood to attention.

I glanced over my shoulder to Diane, who was still out at the car. I edged my way towards the living room, my heart in my mouth.

I almost jumped out of my skin as I saw Robert lying spark out on the sofa.

Diane came up behind me. "What's wrong?"

I nodded at our intruder who was now stirring.

"Uncle Rob!" Diane squealed.

He shot to his feet as though she'd stuck a pin in his backside. "What the…? Oh, sorry. I must've fallen asleep." He glanced about himself guiltily and began straightening the cushions.

"No shit, Sherlock," Diane said.

I turned and scowled at her, shaking my head.

"Well, it's true. What is he even doing here?"

"For your information, snitchy britches, I brought over some groceries for you in an attempt at an apology."

She shrugged. "Yeah, well, you shouldn't be letting yourself in all the time. Can you leave your key behind, please?"

Although I totally agreed with what she was saying, I kept out of it feeling it wasn't my place to interfere.

Robert dug in his pocket and slammed a key on the coffee table. "I'll tell you what. I'll leave you both to it. You've made it perfectly clear you don't want me in your life."

"Robert." I reached out, touching his arm, trying to diffuse the situation.

"No. It's fine. Forget it." He shrugged my hand off. "She knows where I'll be if she changes her mind." He stomped out through the kitchen reminding me of a spoiled toddler.

"Maybe that was a bit harsh?" I said, watching him march to the gate at the bottom of the garden.

"Why? You said you thought he was the one who came in the other night. If we're staying here, I want to be in control of the keys. Don't you?"

I nodded. "Yeah, but I can't help feeling a little sorry for him. For all his faults, he thinks the world of you."

"I'll leave him to calm down, then I'll go and apologise in a day or two."

I opened the fridge. Robert had stocked it with milk and butter. There was a plastic bag filled with a variety of breads and biscuits on the worktop. "Yeah, I think you probably should. His heart's in the right place," I said.

"Can I invite Andre around for a couple of hours?"

"I don't see why not. I need to check my emails and pay a few bills, anyway. Do you know the password for the computer in the office? It'll save me trying to do it on my phone."

"I think so. It used to be *princessdi1*."

"You don't mind if I use it, do you?"

"Of course, I don't." She pulled her phone out of her pocket and began tapping away as she headed upstairs.

I ran my bag up to my room and changed into a T-shirt and a pair of jogging bottoms before trudging back downstairs.

It felt weird going into Eddie's office, but I figured the feeling would lessen once I'd forced myself to do it a few times. The password Diane had recited worked first time. I logged in to my emails and sent a detailed message to Angel. I'd promised to contact her as soon as I'd landed in the UK, but I knew she'd understand. Then I set about paying several Spanish utility bills.

As I was about to log off, a private Facebook message popped up at the bottom, right-hand corner of the screen. It confused me at first as I hadn't logged in to my Facebook account, but then I realised the message wasn't meant for me.

Yo, brother. Not seen you on here in a while.

I clicked on the message. It opened in a larger screen. The sender was a smiley-faced man with ginger dreadlocks called Mannie Walters. I felt suddenly sick. What would I tell him? As I contemplated what to do, my eyes travelled over the previous correspondence between the guy and Eddie. My mouth fell open.

Eddie – *They don't seem to give a toss that I'm the majority shareholder. I started this business from scratch.*

Mannie – *So, why do they want to sell?*

Eddie – *Why do you think? Money. The root of all evil.*

Mannie – *Yeah, but what does it have to do with Robert? He's not even a partner.*

Eddie –*Donald's got into his head. Convinced my greedy brother to side with him.*

Mannie – *Well, it's your call, bro. But don't be forced into anything.*

Eddie – *Over my dead body.*

I gasped. So Donald and Robert wanted to sell the business. It was clear from this conversation that Eddie had been totally against the sale.

I felt as though the air had been sucked from my lungs. This was massive. Eddie had put the mockers on the sale and now he was dead—no longer a problem. Robert was to inherit the business, therefore free to sell. I needed to do something about this. I raced for my phone and took several photographs of the entire conversation.

Hearing Diane on the stairs, I shoved my phone in the pocket of my jogging bottoms, turned off the computer screen and got to my feet meeting her in the hallway.

"Did you manage to log in?" she asked, glancing into the office.

"I did, thanks." I smiled as best I could, worried she'd pick up on my tension. "Is Andre coming over?"

"Yeah. He's on his way."

"Good. I might go and buy something for dinner once he's here. Sound good to you?"

A flash of panic crossed her face, but then she smiled and nodded. "Yeah. Sure."

I busied myself cleaning down the kitchen sink. Then I stared out of the window with a new understanding—at the garden and the adjoining gate.

Could Robert really be responsible for killing Steph and Eddie? *For money?*

The feeling of violation was so complete. My mind jumped straight to default, to worse-case-scenario. It felt as though someone had stomped their way into my mind and trampled on every thought, feeling and emotion. To think I'd stayed under the same roof as such a monster made my insides balk. Bile rose in my throat. I bent over the sparkling clean sink and threw up.

I heard Diane open the front door and Andre's dulcet tones, so I quickly swilled down the sink and slurped some water into my bitter-tasting mouth.

Pasting a smile on my face, I turned as they entered the kitchen.

"You okay, Aunt Susie?" Diane asked, eyeing me suspiciously.

"Sure, I'm fine. Hi, Andre, how are you?"

"I'm good," he said.

"And your mum?"

"She's angry. She received divorce papers this morning. I was glad to get away from her, to be honest."

"I might pop in to see her on the way back from the supermarket. Will you guys be okay on your own for a while?"

"We'll be upstairs playing music. Andre's brought his iPod."

"Okay. I'll be off then. Won't be long." I grabbed my handbag and keys and shot out the front door.

CHAPTER 31

I HAD NO IDEA WHAT I INTENDED TO DO. MY FIRST INSTINCT WAS TO go to Robert and confront him. But I wouldn't be responsible for what I'd do to him. And to think I'd felt sorry for him earlier. However, if I did go around, he'd know I was onto him. That could ruin things for Conrad.

Conrad. That's what I'll do. I'll tell him, and he can deal with it.

I drove out of the street and parked around the corner before ringing the Detective.

"Jenkins," he barked into my ear.

"Conrad, it's Susanna. Can you talk?"

"Yes. What's up?"

"I may have found something, but I don't want Diane finding out until we know for sure."

"Okay. Do you want to meet, or can you tell me over the phone?"

"I'd rather meet. Where are you?"

"I'm tied up for an hour or so. Shall I come to the house?"

"No!" I said quickly. "I'll meet you in town somewhere."

"Okay. Let's make it The Thistle again, if you like?"

"Great. See you in an hour."

I glanced at my watch, 1.20pm. I'd take a trip to the supermarket and then pop in to see Teresa.

I found myself dawdling around the supermarket, unable to focus on anything. It was 2.05pm by the time I piled the bags into the boot, so I drove straight to The Thistle.

"What can I get you?" a sexy young woman asked from behind the bar.

I'd been looking forward to seeing Ryan, but there was no sign of him. "Is there any chance I can get a coffee?"

"Latte?" she asked.

I shrugged. "Sounds good. No Ryan today?"

"He's around somewhere. Do you want me to call him?"

"No. It's fine."

I waited for the girl to make my coffee and then slid into the same booth as last time. Taking my phone from my pocket, I began to read the conversation from scratch again, this time with a clear head.

"I thought it was you." Ryan appeared beside my table, startling me.

My heartbeat faltered. Although not as obviously good-looking as Conrad, something about him appealed to me—a lot. "Oh, hi. Yeah, I'm meeting Conrad for a catch up."

"I see. Any closer to figuring out who did it?"

I screwed up my face and shook my head. "Doesn't look like it."

"Bummer."

"I see you're no longer a one-man band." I nodded at the barmaid who was staring back at us.

"Oh, you met Corinne. Yeah, she's just helping out for a few days."

"She's pretty."

He nodded glancing at the young woman again.

I felt an unexpected twinge of jealousy.

"She's lovely if you like that type."

"And *you* don't?" I realised I was flirting with him dressed in scruffy T-shirt and jogging bottoms while in competition with a gorgeous sex-bomb half my age. What the hell was wrong with me?

"My taste is a little less obvious, if you know what I mean?" He cocked one eyebrow causing my stomach muscles to clench deliciously.

Conrad appeared behind Ryan. I sat upright and straightened my expression.

"Conrad, my man. What can I get for you?" Ryan didn't miss a beat.

Conrad spied my cup and nodded. "Coffee for me too. I'm still on duty."

Ryan winked at me and headed behind the bar.

"So, what do you have for me?" Conrad said as soon as he was seated.

"I had an enlightening conversation with one of Eddie's online contacts." I turned on the phone once again and placed it in front of him.

He whistled. "Can you email these to me?"

"Yes. Of course. And there's more."

"Really? Go on."

"Robert is going to inherit Eddie's share of the business."

Conrad nodded. "You did already tell me that which sets off alarm bells now, to be honest. Anything else?"

"When we were staying at Robert's, Diane said she thought the killer was in her bedroom. We thought she was dreaming, but then another night he burst into my room as he couldn't find Diane who happened to be in with me. I thought it was odd but put it down to him worrying about her."

Ryan appeared with another coffee.

"Cheers, mate," Conrad said, and waited until we were alone before continuing. "So, what changed?"

"The other night, after we'd moved into Steph's house,

someone let themselves in and turned off the alarm. Diane was certain once again that the killer was in her room."

"And you think it was Robert?"

I shrugged tracing a finger around a beer mat. "I don't know. But after reading that message today, it makes me wonder. He had a key and knew the alarm number, so it could've been him."

"I see."

"But I really don't want Diane upset by all of this, if you can help it? If it turns out to be nothing, she still needs a positive relationship with her uncle."

"I get you. Can I trust you to keep it under wraps while I make a few enquiries?"

"Definitely. I hope I'm completely wrong, but, if not, I want that bastard to pay."

"I've been meaning to speak to you," Conrad said. "We've had confirmation from the security firm that oversee your apartment, and apparently the CCTV camera in the main apartment block hasn't been working for a few weeks. They said they'd emailed all the residents about it back in April."

"Really? I haven't received anything—it must've gone to Giles' email. Does this mean I'm a suspect?"

"Well, lucky for you, the cameras in the car park are still working and they confirmed both the cars registered to you hadn't been moved for months, so, for now at least, you're okay."

I exhaled noisily unaware I'd been holding my breath. "Thank goodness for that."

Conrad nodded, took a couple of gulps of his coffee, and then left.

I stayed seated waiting for my heartbeat to return to normal.

"Still fancy going out for dinner one night? Now I have a bit of help around the place, it's easier," Ryan said, approaching me again as soon as he saw Conrad leave.

"Er… yeah, I guess so. If I can get somebody to sit with Diane, of course."

"Of course. And if not, bring her along."

"Really?"

He nodded. "Really. I'd prefer it to be just us, but your niece is cool. I like her."

"Okay then. Let me know when, and I'll see what I can arrange."

I left the bar with a spring in my step. And although I knew I wasn't ready for a relationship yet, I really liked Ryan. The fact he wasn't put off by Diane was a bonus.

Teresa answered the door and her face dropped when she saw me.

"Bad time?"

"No, but look at the state of me."

I glanced at her pink Care Bears pyjamas and laughed. "Look at the state of me, and I've been in a bar looking like this."

"You win. Come on in, I'll pour us a wine." She stepped to the side and allowed me to enter.

I opted for a glass of water and sat opposite her at the small round dining table. "Andre told me you'd had a shock in the mail."

"Cheeky bastard didn't even warn me. Eighteen years of marriage down the swanny without so much as a by your leave."

"Surely you wouldn't want him back though? After everything he's done."

"No way! But it still pisses me off. I actually prayed he would come to miss me so much he'd return with his tail between his legs begging me to take him back."

"And you'd slam the door in his face."

"Got it in one. I don't want the weak prick to be happy. I want him to be miserable."

"You're wasting your time worrying about him. You should be out there, looking for husband number two. Someone who's worthy of you and Andre."

"I can't see that happening. Who'd want me?"

"Hey! Don't talk like that. You're a catch and don't you forget it."

"Thanks, Susanna. I needed this kind of pep talk today. But I don't know if I could start again. All that getting to know each other is overrated."

"Oh, I don't know." I thought of Ryan's cheeky grin, and my heart began to race.

"What was that?" She laughed.

"What?"

"That twinkle in your eye. Is it Robert?"

I almost choked on a gulp of water. "Piss off."

"Oh good, because you can do much better than that weirdo."

"What makes you say that?"

"Der! Just look at you."

"No, I mean what made you call him a weirdo?"

She shuddered. "He called around here one night—said he wanted to get acquainted with Andre's family. He knew I was here alone because Diane had told him."

"Really?"

She nodded. "Don't say anything, will you? He didn't do anything out of order, just gave me the creeps. I was glad when he'd gone."

"I won't say anything. But I know what you mean, to be honest."

"Did he try it on with you?"

"He'd be wearing his testicles as earmuffs if he had."

Teresa snorted. "Gosh, you're funny. I kinda wish he had now just to see his face."

I wanted to confide in her what I'd just discovered, but I'd promised Conrad I wouldn't breathe a word to anybody.

We chatted for an hour or so and then I got to my feet. "I'd best go and see what the love-birds are up to."

"Oh, don't, Susie. That's the last thing we need, an unplanned pregnancy," Teresa said.

I shuddered. "Shit. I never thought about that. I have a lot to learn about parenting a teen. Don't I?"

We hugged like old friends and she waved me off at the doorstep.

When I got back to the car, I noticed I'd missed a call from Robert. Feeling guilty, I was relieved to see he'd left a voicemail message.

The funeral is booked for Thursday. Unless you have any objections that is. Let me know.

His mood sounded no better than it had been at the house earlier, but at least he wasn't calling to give me stick for implicating him as a murderer. I replied by text telling him Thursday was fine.

Although I knew Diane dreaded the funeral as much as I did, I also knew the grieving process wouldn't begin properly until after the funeral. I'd be glad when it was all over, and we could look to our future and whatever that held.

CHAPTER 32

Diane and Andre were lying on the bedroom floor, head to head—their bodies facing in opposite directions, sharing earphones.

I rapped on the door until Andre opened one eye and grinned. He nudged Diane and nodded in my direction.

"Oh, I didn't hear you get back. You were ages," she said.

"I stopped in to see Teresa, and we got nattering. I didn't realise the time. Was everything alright?"

Diane nodded and got to her feet. "I missed you, though. I think I had a panic attack."

"Really?" I asked, glancing at Andre who nodded and stood up as well.

"She got really upset and was struggling to breathe," he said. "I remembered a lad in school used to have panic attacks, so I got her to breathe into a paper bag."

"Well done you." I squeezed his arm. "Are you okay now, sweetie?"

"I think so."

"What caused it?"

"A song. A really sad song," she said quietly.

Tears sprang to my eyes, and I pulled her into my arms. "I know. Music is always the worst trigger with me. But it can be very healing too. There's a fine line. Stick to upbeat songs for a while maybe."

She nodded, and I kissed her forehead.

"I had a call from Robert."

Diane groaned.

"The funeral is on Thursday. Is that alright?"

She closed her eyes and nodded. "I guess so. And then what?"

"What do you mean?"

"School starts next week, and I really can't bear the thought of going back there. Not yet."

"Let's get Thursday over, and then we'll decide where to from there. Now, are you staying for dinner, Andre? I bought plenty."

"I should get back to Mum. I told her I wouldn't be late."

"Good call. I think she's still a bit down in the dumps."

I left them and headed into the kitchen. I put a chicken in the oven and began peeling the potatoes and carrots to go with it.

My nerves were on edge. I wondered how Conrad was getting on with his investigation. Although we had Robert's key, I couldn't bear the thought of him just being at the other end of the garden path.

Andre left a few minutes later.

After seeing him off, Diane came into the kitchen and climbed up onto a stool. "Do you want any help?"

"It's all under control, thanks. Can I get you a drink?"

"What did you get?"

"Tea and coffee, of course."

She groaned.

"And I bought some drinking chocolate, blackcurrant cordial, cola and lemonade."

"Ooh. Can I have a glass of blackcurrant and lemonade, please?"

"Help yourself. How are you feeling now after your wobble today?"

"Okay, I think. I don't even know what happened. I was fine one minute and bawling my eyes out the next."

"Andre must've freaked out."

She giggled. "He was great, actually."

"He's a good lad."

"Do you really like him?"

"Don't be so surprised. Of course, I like him. Why wouldn't I?"

"Because nobody else does. He gets a lot of stick."

"He looks scary, but he's a softy, really. And he thinks the world of you."

"Aunt Susie!" Her face flushed a deep red.

THE NEXT FEW days were taken up with us getting settled in the house and into some sort of routine.

Diane withdrew into herself more and more as Thursday approached. I tried to keep any conversation light and upbeat. I thought it remarkable the way she seemed to be coping with everything. This was her first brush with death and to be having to cope with losing both parents in one go didn't bear thinking about.

On Wednesday morning, Conrad texted me to let me know he'd taken Robert in for questioning. Donald Macy was also back in the country and helping them with their enquiries. I didn't want Diane to find out about it, so I took her into town for the day, clothes shopping.

Conrad called me just after dinner. Meanwhile, Diane had gone down the road to show Talia her new wardrobe.

"How did you get on?"

"We had to release them both. Macy was already in Portugal when the murders took place, and he denied the business was for sale. He did admit he'd discussed it with Eddie, but apparently they all agreed it wasn't the right time to sell."

"And you believe them?"

"I think so. But don't worry, we're still investigating."

"Oh, well. I'm relieved in a way, if I'm being totally honest."

"Yeah, I can imagine. Although that means we're back to square one with the investigation."

"So you have no other leads?"

He exhaled noisily. "Not one."

"I won't tell Diane. She has enough on her mind with the funeral tomorrow."

"Yes. Of course. Me and a couple of team members intend to be there. You never know who might turn up, and that could give us the heads up we need."

"Alright. See you tomorrow then."

I busied myself with a pile of laundry and then went upstairs to pick out an outfit for tomorrow. I felt sick every time I thought about the funeral.

When Diane returned home, I was curled on the sofa in front of the TV. "How did it go?"

"Good. Talia loves my new jeans. She asked her mum to buy her some for her birthday."

"I've thrown jeans away that have fewer tears than them."

She rolled her eyes at me and grinned.

My phone rang, and she picked it up from the coffee table and handed it to me.

"Hello?" I said, not recognising the number.

"Hey, Susanna, it's Ryan."

"Oh, hi. How are you?" I felt my cheeks flush.

Diane began making kissy faces at me, and I turned away, swiping at her to give over.

"Just checking how you're fixed for Saturday? Dinner, as promised."

"Saturday?" I glanced at Diane. "I'll see if I can get someone to stay with Diane."

"I'll be fine," she squawked.

"Or bring her, like we discussed," he said.

"Okay, then. That would be nice. I'll let you know if it's just me or both of us closer to the time."

"Can you text me your address. I'll pick you up at seven?"

"Will do. See you then."

Diane was smirking as I hung up. "You've got a date," she said, sitting down next to me.

"Hardly a date. He said you could come too."

"I'm not going. I'll stay with Andre till you get back."

"Whatever. But it's not a date, so wipe that cheeky grin off your face." I tickled her tummy, and she squirmed on the sofa giggling hysterically.

"I've never known anyone as ticklish as you," I said, once she'd calmed down.

"It's just my tummy. I'm fine everywhere else."

"Now I know what to do if it's getting a bit sad tomorrow." I wriggled my fingers like a crawling spider.

CHAPTER 33

Robert looked terrible when he turned up first thing the next morning. He had his suit in a hanger bag. "Can I get a shower here, please? My water heater's on the blink."

"Of course." I opened the door wider for him to enter. "Diane's in the upstairs bathroom, but the downstairs one's free."

He didn't say another word as he stomped into the bathroom.

I was ready, apart from changing my clothes. I'd woken up early and had a long soak in the bath before straightening my hair and applying a little makeup.

When Robert reappeared, he looked more like his usual self.

"Coffee?" I said, pouring two cups.

He gave a backwards nod and sat on a stool.

"I suppose you heard the police took me in for questioning yesterday?"

I didn't know what Conrad had told him. I just nodded as I handed him a mug.

"I told them they were wasting their time, but it seems they have nothing else to go on so they decided to focus their attention on me."

"Diane doesn't know, so it's probably best we keep it like that," I said. "She has enough to deal with today."

He chewed his bottom lip, staring into his coffee.

"What time will the cars be here?"

"Ten-thirty. How is Diane?"

"Coping. Which is all we can ask for at this stage."

Robert shook his head. "I don't know why she's got it in for me lately."

"Familiarity. She needs to lash out at someone, and it so happens to be you. She'll come around in her own good time."

"How did you become an expert on kids so quickly?"

I was unsure if he was being a sarky prick again, but he seemed to be genuine. "I'm not—I'm winging it." I heard a sound on the stairs and gestured to Robert to alert him Diane was on her way down.

"Hi, Uncle Rob." She kissed her surprised uncle's cheek and wrapped her arms around him, snuggling into his chest.

"Hi, princess."

I noticed his eyes glistened, and I turned away, blinking away my own tears. Today was going to be sad, but I was determined to keep it together for as long as possible. "Orange juice, Diane?" I placed a glass in front of her.

"Thanks," she said sitting down beside Robert. She reached for the glass, her hand shaking.

I glanced at Robert. He'd noticed it too.

"Mum and Dad can't make it." Robert finally broke the heavy silence.

"What a shame. Are they sick?" I asked.

"Dad's been sick for years, but he really wanted to make the effort. However, Mum had a funny turn the other night, and the doctor has advised her not to travel. I mentioned I might take Diane to see them in a few weeks' time."

"That would be lovely. Have you been to Ireland before, Diane?"

She shook her head. "I've always wanted to go."

"Well, there you go, then. Something to look forward to." I leaned forward and rubbed her arm.

She just smiled and chewed at her thumbnail.

"I'll get changed." I raced upstairs and dressed in the black, knee-length dress I'd brought from home and a maroon jacket finished off with a black chiffon scarf tied around my neck.

Downstairs, Diane and Robert were still in the exact same spot, each lost in their own thoughts.

A few minutes more silence was broken by the doorbell. Both Diane and I rushed towards it grateful for the distraction.

Andre and Terri stood on the doorstep dressed in their most sombre clothes. Well, Terri was. Andre looked the same as he always did.

We ushered them inside.

"I didn't know if we were to stay outside with that lot or come in?" Terri said, pointing to a crowd of people on the driveway.

"Oh, I don't even know who they are."

Diane glanced out and waved. "Neighbours. And that guy is Donald Macy." She backed up and closed the door again.

I cringed. "We can't just leave them out there." I said.

"I'll go outside to welcome them." Robert nodded at Terri and scooted past us. "The cars will be here soon, anyway."

"Oh, good." Diane had taken Andre into the living room, so I led Terri into the kitchen.

"How's it going?" Terri asked.

"As you'd imagine. We're all bordering on the edge of hysteria with fake smiles on our faces."

"Yep. Just as I imagined." She did her best fake smile.

I groaned. "I've never wanted something to be over so much in my entire life. But, sorry, I meant to ask how you are after receiving the divorce papers?"

She swiped her hand in front of her face. "Oh, I'm well over that. Good riddance, I say."

Robert appeared in the hallway. "The cars are here."

My heart clenched, and I took several gulps of air before feeling strong enough to face Diane. I knocked lightly and popped my head into the living room. "The cars are here, sweetie."

Diane took Andre's hands. Her eyes appeared red and puffy.

"It's okay. Come on." Andre helped her to her feet, hooking her arm through his.

We walked down the driveway and past the crowd of people that had doubled and out onto the street.

Diane leaned heavily on Andre. He caught her when her legs gave out when she saw the two caskets in the front cars. I ushered everyone, including Andre and Terri, into the funeral car. I wasn't about to separate Diane and Andre. Thankfully, Robert didn't say a word.

The next hour passed in a blur. I remembered focusing on the order of service that Robert must've arranged. The image of Steph and Eddie on the front was a recent one—Eddie's hair looked a lot thinner and Steph a little curvier than I remembered. They looked happy though.

During the service Robert read a poem, his voice cracking halfway through, but he managed to finish it which is more than I could've done. There were no hymns as such, unless you count *All Things Bright and Beautiful,* and *Time to Say Goodbye* played as we left the quaint chapel.

Diane had been sobbing during the service, but had managed to pull herself together as we stood outside to greet the guests—all of whom she seemed to know. I, on the other hand, didn't know any of them.

The wake was held at the golf club Eddie had been a member of. We were the first to arrive. I ordered a straight brandy from the bar and swallowed it down in one needing some assistance to get through the rest of this dreadful day.

Diane and Andre found a seat at the back of the room. I

ordered them some drinks, and a red wine for Terri before joining them.

"Aunt Susie has a date on Saturday," Diane said, as I approached the table.

"It's not a date," I hissed, shaking my head at Terri's upturned, questioning face.

"Tell all?"

It must've been the brandy, because I was giggling as I filled her in on all the details.

"Diane can stay with us. I insist. On one condition."

I narrowed my eyes

"I want to hear every detail when you get back."

After another couple of brandies, and a small plate of food, I thought I'd better circulate. I swept the room and found Robert propping up the bar with the man Diane had pointed out as Donald Macy. "Hi, how's it going?" I said lightly.

Robert gave me a tight-lipped smile. "Have you met Steph's sister, Don? Susanna."

The attractive, grey-haired man extended his hand to me. "No, I haven't had the pleasure. This has been a lovely send off, Susanna. Steph would've been thrilled."

"Yes. It's been great, but it had nothing to do with me, I'm ashamed to say. Robert played a blinder."

Robert gave a genuine smile this time, and his cheeks turned pink. "This was Eddie's favourite place apart from his home. It made sense to hold the wake here. How's Diane holding up?"

"She's better than she was. Glad it's all over, no doubt."

"I'm serious about taking her to Ireland. I was thinking maybe next week," Robert said. "You can come too if you like."

"That's great. Probably exactly what she needs after the past couple of weeks, but I won't come. Thanks though." I carried on doing the rounds making my way back to our table.

My feet were killing me, so I slid off my shoes and rubbed at my temples.

"You tired?" Diane asked.

"A little. How about you?"

"I'm okay. But I want to go home. Do we have to stay any longer?"

"You don't have to do anything. If you really want to get going, we'll get a taxi."

"We'll share a cab with you," Terri said, glancing at Andre. "He's almost asleep. It's been a long day."

I escorted Diane in a final sweep of the room for her to say her goodbyes. It was obvious from Robert's face that he disapproved of us being the first to leave, but it was tough. Diane had coped marvellously well and I didn't intend forcing her to stay any longer than necessary. I flashed him a pissed off look, challenging him to say one word.

He didn't.

CHAPTER 34

The taxi dropped Terri and Andre off on the way home, and I had to wake Diane when we pulled onto our drive. "Come on, love. Let's get you inside to bed."

Half asleep, she staggered inside and upstairs flopping onto her bed fully dressed.

I contemplated whether to try to undress her but decided to leave her be. I removed her shoes, covered her with her duvet, and closed the door quietly.

Downstairs, I made myself a hot drink and watched a bit of TV before heading up to my own bed.

I didn't open my eyes until almost nine the following morning. The first complete night's sleep I'd had in months. When I ventured from my room, I was surprised to find Diane still out for the count and in her own bed. Maybe the funeral was going to be a turning point for us both.

After showering, I headed to the kitchen and prepared something to eat.

Diane appeared a short while later and seemed well rested and in good spirits.

"Blueberry and banana pancakes?"

"Yum!" she said, taking a seat at the breakfast bar.

"You sleep okay?"

"Like a log. I don't even remember getting home."

"I could tell you were sleepwalking," I laughed. "It was a long day."

"I'm glad it's over," she said, almost to herself. "But it was a nice day, really. Don't you think?"

"It was a lovely send-off. Your parents had a lot of friends."

She sighed sadly. "Yeah, they did."

I handed her a plate of pancakes smothered in juicy looking blueberries and freshly sliced banana. She snapped out of her melancholy mood.

"Wow! I should take a pic of that and put it on Facebook."

"Really? Don't you get sick of people putting photos of food on there?"

She shrugged and laughed. "Yeah, I do, I guess. But these look better than at a restaurant."

"Give over, you silly sausage. They're pancakes."

"Well, I like them." She shoved a huge forkful into her mouth and grinned, rolling her eyes in mock ecstasy.

I finished cooking my own and sat beside her.

"Are you looking forward to your date tomorrow night?" she asked.

I wrinkled my nose. "Not sure, really. Although it's hardly a date. He said I could bring you along."

"Of course, it's a date. Give me another reason why he would ask you out for dinner. He wants to hook up with you."

"Hook up?" I shuddered and swallowed a mouthful of pancake.

"Okay, so what would you call it then? Grandma used to call it courting?"

"Hook up is definitely too modern for me, but courting is practically ancient."

"Go on, then. What would you call it?"

That stumped me. I didn't have a clue what I would call it.

"We're going out for dinner—end of. It's not a date, and I definitely don't intend hooking up with him."

She wiggled her eyebrows comically. "If you say so."

"Give over, you." I laughed. "We're friends. That's all. Are you sure you'll be alright, though?"

"I'll be fine. You need a life, and I need to get back to normal."

Once again, the wisdom of her words blew me away. "We'll get there, sweetie. And you are my life now and don't forget it."

"I know." She placed the fork down and pushed the plate away from her as though suddenly no longer hungry.

"You've had enough?" I eyed the half-eaten food.

"Yes. It was really nice though."

On Saturday afternoon, I began to get butterflies in my stomach. I contemplated calling Ryan to cancel.

"It's only dinner," Diane teased. "And, besides, Terri will be here to pick me up in a few minutes, so what else are you gonna do?"

I rubbed my forehead and groaned.

"Just go. You'll have a good laugh."

I continued painting my fingernails. "I wish I'd gone for a manicure—this looks rubbish."

"Here, let me help." She took the polish from me. "Does this mean you're going?"

"I guess. But I won't be out late."

"It doesn't matter. Teresa said I can stay there the night."

"It's probably best you don't. You're too young to have a sleepover at your boyfriend's."

"Aunt Susie!" She looked at me with disgust.

"What? I'm only thinking about you."

"It's not like that with Andre. He respects me."

I exhaled in a controlled blow and lifted my eyebrows.

"What's that supposed to mean?"

"I like Andre, you know I do. But I haven't met one teenage boy yet who isn't fixated on sex."

"You have now. We've discussed it, and we decided to wait until I'm sixteen."

"Really?"

She nodded and continued painting my nails.

"That's not far off. Do you need to go on the pill?"

"No. I told you."

"I know what you told me, but I've also been a teenager and I know how these things can just happen. A bit of a snog can lead to a fumble and then before you know it…"

"Gross! I promise you, if I think we're getting close to… you know, I'll tell you."

"I hope you feel as though you can. I'll never judge you. I've been there myself, don't forget."

A car horn sounded outside on the drive.

Diane jumped to her feet. "They're here. What about your other hand? Shall I ask them to come in and wait?"

"No, don't be silly. You go. If I come home early I'll call you and see if you want me to pick you up, okay?"

"Uh-huh." She kissed me on the cheek. "Have a great time. Don't do anything I wouldn't do."

I swatted her behind with my dry hand as she shot away from me laughing.

I finished my nails and ran a deep bubbly bath. I had two hours to kill before Ryan was due and I intended to make the most of them.

It seemed strange to be alone in the house my sister and her husband were butchered in just a couple of weeks ago, but I slid into the bubbles, stuffed my earphones in my ears with the husky tones of Amy Winehouse playing, and closed my eyes trying to block out the chatter of my brain.

An hour later, wrapped in my robe, I began applying a full face of make-up, and then I straightened my hair within an inch of its life. I looked pretty damn good even if I did say so myself.

Choosing a burnt-orange coloured dress and strappy sandals, I stood in front of the mirror, pleased with my reflection. I didn't know what Ryan had in mind, but my dress, although classy, wouldn't look out-of-place anywhere—unless he had a game of bowls in mind, of course.

The doorbell chimed, and, after a final dab of lipstick, I ran downstairs, suddenly giddy.

CHAPTER 35

Ryan had his back to the door as I opened it. He took my breath away when he slowly turned around. His familiar cheeky grin put me at ease right away.

"Wow! You scrub up well," I said, looking him up and down. He was dressed in a pale grey single-breasted suit, black brogues, white shirt, and black tie.

"Not as well as you!" He practically drank me in with his eyes. "So, are you ready?"

"One minute." I grabbed my jacket and handbag from the bottom of the stairs, set the alarm, and met him out on the doorstep.

"Just the two of us, then?" He held his arm out like a gentleman.

"Yes. Diane said she didn't want to play gooseberry."

"Top girl."

He opened the door of his flash deep-blue Mazda. He waited until I was seated before striding around to the driver's side.

"I could get used to being treated like this." I winked at him.

"I'm nothing if not a gentleman."

"So, where are you taking me?"

"I made a reservation at the new Thai restaurant in Penrith."

"Ooh, sounds lovely."

"You do like Thai food, then?"

"I love it. Not that I've had it very often, mind you."

He backed out the drive and turned towards the motorway. "I've *never* tried it."

"Seriously? Then why choose Thai?"

"It sounds classier than a kebab." He cocked one comical eyebrow at me.

"Yes. That's right. It does sound classier than a kebab. Although, there's nothing better than a greasy kebab at the end of a boozy night."

"Oh, the woman of my dreams." He placed a hand in the centre of his chest as though steadying his heartbeat.

I was going to enjoy the evening if the last five minutes were anything to go by.

Fifteen minutes into the half-hour journey, my phone rang. My heart raced as I rummaged in my bag and yanked it out. A number I didn't recognise flashed across the screen.

"Hello?"

"Hi, Susanne. It's Terri. Sorry to bother you."

"What's wrong?"

"Oh, no. Nothing's wrong. It's just that the kids want to watch an R18 film and I thought I'd best ask you first."

"Oh. I don't really know what to say. Are you okay with it?"

"I am, but it's okay if you'd rather she didn't watch it."

"No. If you don't mind then I'm alright with that."

"Fab. How's it going?"

I felt myself blush as I glanced at Ryan and gave him an *I'm sorry* shrug. "I can't talk right now, Terri. I'll call you tomorrow."

She gasped. "Is he there with you? Oh, I'm so sorry. Have a great night."

The phone went dead in my ear.

Ryan laughed.

"Did you hear that?"

"Every word."

I giggled. "It's Diane's boyfriend's mum. She's lovely but ever so slightly mad."

"Aren't we all?"

"So, who's looking after the hotel tonight?" I asked.

His smiling face suddenly clouded over. "Long story. I'll tell you later. I don't want to think about it right now."

"Oh, okay. Sorry."

He reached for my hand. "Don't be sorry. I just want to focus on you tonight. Tell me about your place in Spain. Whereabouts is it?"

"Three hours outside of Malaga, a lovely little village called Arenas Blancas. Have you heard of it?"

He shook his head. "No, but I've been to Malaga. It's a lovely place. I'd like to go again one day. But I'd stay longer than a fortnight next time. Can't really get a true feel for a place when you're a tourist."

"I know what you mean. My village is probably one of the few places left in Spain that hasn't been hammered by tourism, but I'm sure it's only a matter of time. Hard to keep such a beautiful place under wraps, but I would if I could."

"Maybe you'll show it to me one day?"

I rolled my eyes and chuckled. "A little forward, aren't you? This is only our first date."

"Who said anything about it being a date?" He looked at me, horrified.

My heart dropped. "I didn't... I mean..."

He burst out laughing. "Of course, it's a date. I'm only teasing you."

I couldn't help joining in with his infectious laughter even though I felt a little silly.

We pulled into a carpark on the outskirts of Penrith town

centre. Minutes later we were seated opposite each other in a booth.

We had a lovely evening, and the time flew by.

"Thanks so much for tonight, Ryan," I said, sipping the last of my wine. "I've really enjoyed myself for the first time in ages. I'm sad it's over, to be honest."

"It's not over yet." He motioned for the waiter. "Fancy a coffee?"

I nodded offering him a grateful smile.

"I suppose I'd better tell you what's been happening with me and the hotel, hadn't I?"

"Only if you want to." I wanted more than anything to know what was wrong but didn't want to appear pushy.

He rubbed his face with both hands as though having a dry wash. "I told you my wife left, didn't I?

Well, we were joint partners in the business, fifty-fifty. She's been trying to make me sell up, no doubt for her fancy man to get his hands on her money, but I've refused up to now. She's been getting at the staff hence the staffing issues, and just trying to make my life miserable in any way possible."

"That's terrible!" I stroked the back of his hand.

"You haven't heard the best bit yet."

The waiter appeared with our coffee.

Ryan inhaled deeply once we were alone again. "Last week, my lovely ex took things one step further. She moved back in bringing the boyfriend with her."

"No!"

He nodded. "She's insisting on staying until I either buy her out or sell up."

"What are you going to do?"

"I honestly don't know. Since she's come back, we're suddenly fully staffed again. She's trying to wind me up with the boyfriend, but I honestly don't care anymore. She means nothing to me."

"Can't you buy her out?"

"I could. But I don't think I want to."

"Then sell up."

"That's the only way forward, if I'm being honest. But I just want to make her wait. Why should she get everything her own way?"

"But she's going to, anyway. You might as well get it over and done with, and then you can get on with the rest of your life."

"I know. You're right. And I will. But I'll do it in my own time, not when she demands it."

"Are you sure you're not still hung up on her?"

He blurted out a laugh. "You've got to be joking. We were together seven years, but I don't think either of us were happy for more than half of them."

"Maybe she did you a favour then?"

"Yeah. I know. But there's just something about that smug face that makes me want to pummel it into the ground."

"Your wife's face?"

He chuckled, a rich, warm rumble that came from the centre of his chest. "No. Her boyfriend, of course."

"Oops. That's what I meant."

He rolled his eyes. "Whatever."

I glanced around the restaurant. "I think they're waiting to close up," I said, indicating the waiters hovering by the till.

"Come on, then. Have you finished?"

I drained the last of my coffee and got to my feet.

While Ryan went to pay, I rummaged in my handbag for my phone. It wasn't there. In a panic I upended my bag on the table.

"What's wrong?"

"My phone. It's not here."

"Did you leave it in the car?"

"I hope so. I told Diane I'd call her when we were on our way home in case she wants picking up."

I found the phone down the side of my seat in the car.

I gasped when I looked at the screen. Six missed calls. With bumbling fingers, I listened to the first of the messages.

Susanne, it's Terri. Seems the kids had an argument and Diane stormed off home. I've been over there, and there's no sign of her. Sorry about this, love. I could bang their bloody heads together.

I hung up, feeling as though my heart had stopped. I clapped my hand to my mouth, struggling to breathe.

CHAPTER 36

Furious, Diane raced from Andre's house.

At the end of the path, she heard him calling for his mum and knew they'd be out in the car any second now. Instead of turning right, she turned left knowing he wouldn't think to look for her that way.

She crossed the road keeping to the shadows. Her heartbeat thundered in her ears.

She roared into the night—a strangled, empty noise that sounded more like a whimper.

Aunt Susie would be annoyed with her for going home alone, but how could she stay and listen to Andre's fucking lies. They'd been having a great time until he let it slip that Uncle Rob had been arrested for murdering her parents. Why had nobody told her? It wasn't as if it didn't fucking affect her.

She tried to defend her uncle, of course, but Andre went on and on. He said Uncle Rob wanted to get his hands on her dad's business so he could sell it to some big company.

She'd slapped his face and ran, unable to listen to one more lying word.

She stepped backwards, tight to the treeline when Andre and his mum sped from the garage.

She ran down a side street and towards Robert's house, planning to sneak through the gate at the bottom of his garden.

She pulled her jacket around herself against the bracing wind. As her temper cooled, she suddenly felt vulnerable and scared. The trees surrounding her made the eerie swishing sound from the film they'd just watched. And then she smelled it.

She spun around trying to find where it was coming from.

A gate clanged shut causing her to cry out.

She began to run.

He was following her. She heard the cough. Why the hell did she leave on her own?

She ran on. Her panicked breath sounded like thunder in her ears. Screams locked in her throat.

As she approached Robert's house, she could hear the heavy footfalls on the pavement behind her. One heavier than the other, just like she'd remembered it. She snatched her phone from her pocket and hit redial.

Voicemail.

"He's after me. Please help me," she screamed into the phone.

She turned into Robert's driveway, ran to the front door and hammered both hands on the door. All the lights were turned off and there was no sign of anybody inside.

Whimpering, she headed down the side of the house praying the man didn't know about the gate.

"What's wrong?" Ryan said, easing the car out onto the road.

"It's Diane. She left her boyfriend's, and now they can't find her."

The next message almost gave me a heart attack.

"Oh, my God, Ryan. She's being chased. She said the killer's chasing her."

"Hey, calm down. Is there anyone you can call?"

"Conrad," I shrieked. I dialled his number and spewed out a mass of words as he answered the phone.

"I'm on my way," Conrad said.

I turned to Ryan. "Please hurry. I need to get back there. Diane needs me."

CHAPTER 37

THE STUPID BITCH HAD GONE. SHE'D SENSED I WAS THERE AND BEGAN running off as if her arse was on fire. But there was no sign of her now.

A light flicking on startled me as a man opened the door. I picked up a loose edging tile and held it beside my leg as I approached him.

"What is all the banging about? What are you doing around here at this time of night?"

I shoved him backwards feeling a little off kilter. I preferred the element of surprise to work in my favour.

"Hey! For fuck's sake," he bellowed.

I stepped over the threshold and raised my hand, crashing it down on his head with all my might.

He toppled backwards, a surprised expression on his face. His hand flew to his head. Then, as though in slow motion, he turned and began to scramble away on all fours.

I laughed and kicked him up his backside the same as I'd done to his equally stupid brother. Then I stood above him and smashed the tile into his head once again.

WE COULD SEE the line of red and blue lights as soon as we turned onto the street.

Ryan pulled to a stop as close as he could get.

I jumped from the car and ran towards the house.

A uniformed policewoman tried to stop me at the door.

"I live here," I cried, shoving past her.

"Susanna," Conrad said, halfway down the stairs.

"Did you find her?"

He nodded and walked down to meet me. "She was in a bit of a state, but she's fine. She said she'd been chased all the way home, and once inside, she set the alarm and, hid in her wardrobe. We forced the back door in and woke up the neighbourhood when the alarm sounded."

"Where is she now?"

"Still upstairs. We've searched the grounds, and we can't find anything untoward."

"Do you think she imagined it again?"

"She's definitely shaken up. Just because there's no sign of anything doesn't mean she wasn't chased."

Ryan stepped into the hallway behind us. "Hey, buddy," he said to Conrad. Then he turned to me. "Is she okay?"

"Yes. She's in her bedroom. Do you mind if I go up? I need to see her." I left the men talking and ran upstairs.

Diane burst into tears when she saw me and launched herself into my arms.

"Hey, hey, sweetie. It's okay. I'm here now."

I sat with her for a few minutes and then went back downstairs to see what was happening. Ryan was fixing the back door, and all the cops had gone.

"Oh, hello. Are you alone?"

"Conrad said he'd call you tomorrow. He's left a car outside to keep a look out."

"Do you think you can fix it?" I nodded at the door.

"A temporary fix for tonight. I'll be able to do a proper job in the morning once the shops are open."

"Thanks so much. And thanks for tonight too. I really enjoyed myself."

"How's Diane?"

"She's a mess. Swears it was the same man. She even ran to her uncle's house, but he wasn't bloody in. Poor girl almost died with fright."

"Do you want me to stay over? I can get my head down on the sofa. No funny business, I swear."

I almost hugged him. "Aren't you needed back at the hotel?"

He shrugged. "Stuff 'em. They think they can run it on their own, so let them have a taster."

"Well, if you're sure you don't mind. It would make me feel a little safer.

"That's sorted then. I'll finish securing the door and make us all a cup of tea, shall I?"

It felt good to have another adult to lean on. A sudden feeling of loss gripped my core. Ryan was a good substitute, but he wasn't Giles, and, although he was willing to help out tonight, he would be gone again tomorrow.

"What's wrong?" Ryan asked.

"Oh, nothing."

"Don't give me that. I can tell something's on your mind."

I smiled sadly. "You can read me so well considering we've only known each other five minutes?" I inhaled deeply before continuing. "I was just thinking how grateful I am you're here. It's been a long time since I had another person looking out for me."

He rubbed my arm. "You've had a tough time of it lately, haven't you?"

Tears pricked my eyes, and I quickly turned away not wanting him to see how vulnerable I was.

"Hey, what is it?" He put his arms around me. I allowed him to hug me close to him. I could hear the sound of his steady heartbeat. "I'm here now, so don't you be worrying. Okay?"

I nodded. "Thanks, I really do appreciate it."

"Go and check on Diane. Don't worry about things down here. I'll sort it."

AFTER OFFERING RYAN MY BED, I spent the night in Diane's room. She slept fitfully, and I comforted her well into the early hours worried she would have another anxiety attack.

Waking early, I slid out of bed and padded downstairs barefoot. Moments later, the creaking of floorboards above my head told me I would soon have company. I filled the coffee pot and ran into the bathroom to tidy myself up and brush my teeth. I didn't want to put Ryan off me so soon.

He was already in the kitchen fiddling with the back door when I returned.

"Oh, you are up," he said.

"Yeah, just. I'm making a coffee. Fancy one?"

"Would I? I've normally had a bucket load by now."

"Oh, I forgot. You're normally up to do the breakfast shift, aren't you?"

"Yep. I wonder how they got on without me this morning."

"Have they called?"

He shrugged. "Don't know. I left my phone in the car. Let them stew. I've been running that place single-handedly for weeks while she was swanning around with her fancy man."

Once again, the sound of movement from above alerted me. Diane was awake. I poured her a glass of orange juice. Just as I was contemplating taking it up to her, she was coming down the stairs.

"Hey, love," I said, as she joined us in the kitchen. "How're you feeling?"

She shrugged and climbed onto a stool.

I placed the glass in front of her. "Shall I make you something to eat? Scrambled eggs? Pancakes?"

"I'm not hungry."

I stroked her arm. "Do you want to tell me what happened? Why did you leave Andre's like that?"

She glanced at Ryan self-consciously.

"Right then." Ryan picked up his car keys. "I'll head to the shops and buy what I need to fix the door. Won't be too long."

Diane waited until the front door had closed behind him. "Why didn't you tell me they'd arrested Uncle Rob?"

My stomach clenched. "Because they let him go without charging him."

"Did you know he'd been trying to make Dad sell the business?"

"I had heard that, but I don't know how true it is," I lied.

"I need to see him. Will you come with me?"

I nodded. "If you're sure. I don't want you working yourself up unnecessarily. It's just not worth it."

"I won't. I just need to ask him to his face. I'll know if he's lying."

"Let's go and get dressed then."

We were dressed and back in the kitchen ten minutes later.

I texted Ryan to tell him we wouldn't be long if he returned before us.

"We can walk through the garden," Diane said, nodding at the back door.

CHAPTER 38

"Have you heard from Andre this morning?" I asked as we made our way along the path and through the gate to the back of Robert's house.

Diane shook her head. "No. And I don't want to. I was on his side when that cop arrested him, yet he was laughing last night accusing Uncle Rob of all sorts."

"I'm sure he didn't mean anything by it. Some people just don't think before they speak."

"I don't care. I'm over it. I'm over him."

I rolled my eyes and smiled. "You'll be best friends before the end of the day. You watch."

"I won't. I saw him for what he really is last night, and I didn't like it."

We rounded the front of Robert's house and Diane knocked on the door and rang the bell.

No answer.

"He might have gone into work."

She shook her head. "Not on a Sunday."

She knocked again and bent to peek through the letter box.

I went to knock on the living room window.

A muted cry coming from Diane made me whirl around to find her slumped on the doorstep, a stricken expression on her face.

"What is it, sweetie? What's happened?"

She looked at me as though she couldn't comprehend my words.

I dropped to my knees beside her and looked in through the letter box too.

A huge streak of blood went from just behind the doorway and spread up the hall. I could see one bare foot from my position at the door, but I was certain whoever the person was they were dead.

I forced myself to my feet and fumbled in my pocket for my phone. Then I rang the last number dialled. Conrad answered on the first ring, and I calmly told him where we were and what had happened.

When I hung up, I pulled Diane into my arms. I don't know how long we stayed that way before Conrad and his team arrived closely followed by an ambulance.

They wasted no time assisting us to our feet and moving us out of the way before smashing their way inside.

I tried to see, but it was pointless, and Diane needed me so I walked her back the way we came.

Ryan was already at the house waiting for us, and my legs almost buckled underneath me as I saw him.

Rapid tears ran down my face. "Oh, Ryan. Help me, please."

Clearly confused, he rushed to our side and helped me get Diane inside and onto the sofa.

In a strange trance-like state again, she sat where we placed her and stared at nothing, as though not even aware of our presence.

"What happened?" Ryan asked.

Swallowing the dread constricting my throat, I scrunched my

brows together and shook my head. "I think Robert's been attacked."

"You think?"

"Someone's been attacked in Robert's house. I couldn't see who it was."

"Fuck! And you both found him? I'll make us all a hot drink. Be right back." Ryan rushed from the room.

I was so grateful he was there. Just the mere fact I wasn't the only adult present shared the burden somewhat.

"You okay, sweetie?"

Diane stared at a spot on the wall just above the mantelpiece and didn't say a word.

"I've decided I'm going to take you to Spain. You shouldn't have to be dealing with all this, my love."

"Who's going to Spain?"

I looked up as Ryan placed a tea tray on the table.

"Me and Diane. We can't stay here while there's a lunatic on the loose. I'll take her to my villa. Nobody knows where it is, and we'll be safe there."

"When will you go?"

"Today, if I can arrange flights. Can I leave you with her a second while I go check the website?"

Within half an hour, I'd booked two flights to Malaga leaving just before midnight. I needed to get my skates on if we were going to make it on time.

The doorbell rang as I was cramming our clothes in two cases. I ran downstairs just as Ryan opened the door, allowing Conrad inside.

"Was it Robert?" I asked, leaving him standing in the hall.

He nodded.

My hand flew to my mouth. "What happened?"

"He'd been hit with a brick by all accounts. SOCO are examining the scene, and it appears they've found what they suspect is the weapon."

"Poor Robert. Why would someone want to kill him?"

"He's not dead."

"He's not? Oh, thank God for that. Is he going to be okay?"

"Who can tell? He's in good hands now. I'll let you know if I hear anything. How's Diane?"

"Not good. She's gone again. You know, away with the fairies."

"Maybe you should get her checked out?" Conrad said.

"What's the point? It's shock. She'll be okay in a day or two. I'll let her know Robert's not dead. That might help." I rubbed my tired eyes. "We could only see his foot and thought the worst."

"Do you have any suspects, Conrad?" Ryan asked.

"Early days. We'll want to talk to Andre again in light of the argument he and Diane had last night over Robert."

"Did she tell you what it was over?"

Conrad nodded. "She told one of my officers, yes."

"And you think it could be Andre after all?"

He arched his eyebrows. "Like I say, early days, but we'll keep you up to date."

"Thanks, Conrad. And thanks for last night too. I didn't know who else to call."

"No problem. That's my job. Talking of which, I'd best be off." He turned and left.

"I didn't even ask him in," I said, realising we were still standing in the hallway.

"Don't worry about it. Did you sort the flights out?" Ryan asked.

"I did. I managed to get us on the eleven-fifty flight tonight."

He looked at his watch. "Shit, you'll need to hurry up. Do you want me to drive you to the airport? I don't mind."

"No. Thanks anyway, but I'll drop my car off at the apartment and get a cab from there."

He tipped his head backwards in acknowledgment. "Ah, I forgot you had an apartment in Manchester. I'll let you get on with it while I secure this back door for you."

"Thanks so much, Ryan. I bet this has been your most memorable first date ever."

"You can say that again. I'll be dining out on this story for the rest of the year."

I laughed. "You're such a twit."

Diane still hadn't moved a muscle.

"Hey, darling. Detective Jenkins called in. Robert's still alive."

Her eyes flickered momentarily.

"That's right. He's not dead. He's in hospital." I waited for my words to sink in but there was no further response. "I'm just packing our things. I'm taking you to Spain for a while. Okay, sweetie? I won't be long."

CHAPTER 39

Diane still hadn't said a word when we arrived in Manchester. When I asked her to do something, she went through the motions, as though she could hear me, yet she didn't respond verbally at all.

"Come on. We'll check out the apartment and then call a cab. We need to be at the airport with lots of time to spare." I ran around the car and opened her door. She got out and followed me to the lift.

"Do you know where we're going, Diane?"

Nothing.

"I'm taking you to my villa in Spain. You'll love it there. We'll sunbathe and swim in the sea. It'll do us both the world of good."

Not a flicker. Was she just ignoring me?

Everything was as we'd left it in the apartment.

I called a cab and ran to the bathroom to freshen up. When I came out, Diane was standing beside the window looking out towards the city.

"I've been here before," she said, sounding drugged.

"Yes, Diane. This is my apartment in Manchester. Do you remember?"

She turned and nodded.

"We're going away for a few days. Is that alright?"

"To Manchester?"

"No, sweetie. We're in Manchester to drop the car off, and then we're going to the airport. I'm taking you to Spain."

"Spain?"

I nodded, feeling a little jittery. Maybe I should've had her seen by the doctor. "Yes. We'll have a wonderful time—just the two of us."

"Not Uncle Rob?"

I brushed the palm of my hand along the dusty bookshelf trying to appear casual. "No. Not this time." I wasn't sure if she remembered what we'd seen earlier, but now she was talking, I didn't want to jeopardize anything.

The intercom buzzed.

"Right. Come on, the cab's here. Do you need to use the bathroom before we go?"

She walked to the bathroom as though we had all the time in the world, but I figured she must be busting to go to the toilet after being spaced out all day.

She reappeared a few minutes later, still not all there. I would have to take her to the doctor in Malaga if she was no better by tomorrow.

Once in the cab, I used my phone to book into the Malaga Airport Holiday Inn Express, somewhere I used to stay with Giles whenever we arrived on a late flight. Then I called Angel.

She sounded half asleep when she picked up.

"Did I wake you, Angel? I'm sorry."

"You didn't wake me. I'm reading."

"Oh, good. Listen, I'm on my way to the airport. Is there any chance you and Marvin can pick us up in the morning? I've booked into the Holiday Inn."

"You're coming home?"

The fact that Angel had called my villa home brought a rush of tears to my eyes. "Yes. For now, at least. I'm bringing my niece with me."

"We'll leave at daybreak," Angel said, her excitement evident in her voice. "Oh, and Susanna, I'm so very happy."

"So am I, Angel. See you tomorrow."

I'D HOPED Diane would've perked up a bit once we arrived at the airport, but she didn't. It was as though a protective woollen blanket had been thrown over her emotions.

We'd had a message from Conrad to say Robert was in a stable condition although still unconscious. I wondered what he'd say once he discovered Diane, and I had left the country. But I couldn't think of anybody else right now. My main concern was getting Diane out of danger.

Ryan promised to keep an eye on the house while we were gone, and I gave him permission to stay there if things got too heavy at the hotel with his ex and her fancy man.

With everything that had gone on, I hadn't had a chance to ponder on how I really felt about Ryan. But I was aware my heartbeat quickened whenever I thought about him.

As we boarded the plane, I reached out for Diane's hand hoping for some sign as to how she was feeling. Even after all the years jetting here, there and everywhere, I still got butterflies when I stepped on a plane.

Nothing.

"You okay, sweetie?"

She nodded. Deadpan.

Five minutes after take-off, Diane closed her eyes, and I had no way of knowing if she was asleep or not. She seemed calm enough.

I attempted to watch a comedy episode, but I couldn't follow it. My mind was wandering all over the place. I closed my eyes for the remainder of the flight.

I shook Diane gently just before the pilot prepared to land. She opened her eyes with a start, clearly distressed.

"I'm sorry. I didn't mean to frighten you. Are you okay?"

She nodded and looked out of the tiny window at the dark night and millions of tiny lights below. "Are we here already?"

"Yes. You were zonked the entire flight. Do you feel a little better?"

"I don't know what I feel, if I'm honest. But I am relieved I'm far away from whoever it is trying to kill my family."

"Nobody knows where we are now. You'll be totally safe at the villa I promise you."

She gulped nervously and turned back to the window.

It was only natural for her to be unsure, but a day or two skimming shells into the ocean and strolling along the secluded beaches and she'd begin to relax. I was certain of it.

We only had carry-on luggage, so we were through customs and piling into a taxi in record time. Although I'd manage to get some sleep on the plane, I was exhausted and ready for my bed.

ANGEL AND MARVIN arrived a little after ten the next morning just as Diane and I were tucking into our breakfast.

Angel gave me the biggest hug and, once again, brought me to tears. Apart from Diane, Angel was the closest person I had to family now. I introduced her to Diane, and she sat with us, ordering coffees for her and Marvin. He'd toddled off in the direction of the toilets. I could tell she was dying to quiz me about everything, but I knew she wouldn't while Diane was in earshot.

Although still a little subdued, Diane seemed a lot better than yesterday. She'd eaten a small pastry, and drank a full glass of orange juice for breakfast, which was a good sign she was getting back to normal.

Once Angel and Marvin had been refreshed with two cups of coffee each, we loaded our cases into their car and set off for the villa.

Angel chattered nonstop on the journey.

Diane grinned at me as if to say, *doesn't she ever stop for a breath?*

I squeezed her hand playfully.

Then Diane gasped—we'd reached the coast road and the vast open blueness of the Alboran Sea.

"Beautiful, isn't it?"

She nodded, gazing in awe at the breathtaking view. It never lost its charm for me.

After an hour, Diane leaned against me and fell asleep.

CHAPTER 40

I WANTED TO CRY AS I BURST IN THROUGH THE DOOR OF MY LOVELY villa. The place had been my sanctuary after Giles had died, and I was thrilled to be back in the comfort and security of its four walls.

"Where shall I put my bag?" Diane asked, a smidgen of excitement behind her eyes.

"There are only two bedrooms, but there's a box-room at the back of the villa that could be a bedroom at a push."

She chose the bedroom next to mine.

Angel and Marvin had dropped off our things and left to go for a siesta.

"Let's unpack, then I'll take you for a walk along the beach. Afterwards, we can go into town to pick up some groceries and maybe grab some lunch. What do you think?"

"What kind of things can you buy here? Is it all shellfish? I don't like shellfish."

"Lots of exciting and yummy food, don't worry. You won't go hungry. I promise."

I unpacked my bag and then stripped off the beds ready to remake them with fresh linen after our walk.

"You ready?" I called, before stepping out onto the veranda. I was so happy to be home, and that feeling made me realise where my heart lay. Yet I had no idea how I could make it work.

Diane appeared beside me dressed in a pretty lemon-coloured dress.

"Gosh, you look nice." I'd found the dress in her wardrobe and packed it on the off chance, although I hadn't seen her in anything other than grey and black before.

"Mum bought it in the sales at the beginning of summer. This is the first time I've had it on."

"Well, you look fantastic. Maybe we can go shopping for some more while we're here? It's far too hot for jeans and T-shirts all the time."

"Okay. I think I've out-grown the goth stuff anyway."

I linked my arm through hers and led her down the steep steps to the beach.

"I like it here," she said.

"Me too. It's a completely different life isn't it? Like all that nasty stuff has happened to someone else's family—not ours."

She nodded. "Can we pretend it didn't happen? Never speak of it again?"

"If that's what you want, we can. For now, at least."

She nodded and gazed out at sea.

"Have you heard anything from Andre?"

She nodded. "He texted earlier."

"Are you friends again?"

"Kind of. It wasn't really his fault. But I don't think I want to be his girlfriend anymore."

"Have you gone off him?"

"No. I just don't think I can care about anybody else right now. I want to focus on me."

"Sometimes you sound very grown up, you know? You astound me. Did you tell him where we are?"

"Yes."

"Diane! I told you not to tell anyone. We can't afford to trust anybody until the killer is caught."

"And you think it's Andre?"

"I'm not saying that, but what if he tells someone else?"

"He won't—he promised. I also told him I wouldn't be back for school next week—if ever."

"And how do you think you'll feel if we don't go back? Is that actually an option?"

She shrugged again, then bent to pick up a tiny, pearl-white shell. "I can't face going back there right now. But who knows? Maybe I'll change my mind after a while."

"Yes. We'll give ourselves a couple of weeks and then decide what we want to do."

"Is the beach always this secluded?"

"Not always. But most of the time it is. It gets busier further up closer to the village."

"And are there actually any kids my age around here?"

I laughed. "Of course, there are. But you'll probably have to learn Spanish."

"Don't they speak English?" She looked appalled.

"We're in Spain, sweetie. You may find the odd person knows a little English, but you'll have to learn Spanish if you want to go to school here."

"Really?"

"Well, there're probably English-speaking schools in the city, but I've heard it's best for expats to go to the local schools. They even offer intense language courses to non-Spanish speaking students."

"I don't think I could speak another language. I'm rubbish at French. It's my worse subject at school."

"Well, let's not worry about that yet. I want you to relax and recharge your batteries."

"Have you heard how Uncle Robert is?"

"Not today. I'll call through to the hospital later on."

We strolled in silence for a while before turning back.

"We should go for lunch first before everywhere closes for siesta."

"What's siesta?"

"In Spain it's traditional to have a nap during the hottest part of the day. Most places close for a couple of hours in the afternoon."

"Really? So they go home and have a sleep and then go back to work?"

I nodded.

"What if they don't live close to work?"

"I don't know. I haven't really thought about it. Maybe they get forty winks in the staff room."

We reached the villa and climbed the steps set in the rocks.

I grabbed my handbag and led Diane out to the car shed.

"Oh, it's a nice car," she exclaimed when she saw the almost new metallic blue Nissan Qashqai parked inside.

"Of course, it's a nice car. What were you imagining?"

"When I saw the rickety shed, I expected a scruffy old wreck."

I laughed. "Yeah, the shed needs an overhaul, but it does an adequate job for now. It's stronger than it looks. Get in. Let's go for a quick tour."

CHAPTER 41

Five minutes later we arrived in the quaint ancient village.

Diane was mesmerised with the higgledy-piggledy buildings and narrow cobbled streets. "It's so cute. Like some of the pictures on my screen saver."

"What do you fancy to eat?"

"A burger."

"You won't find your usual fast-food outlets in the village, but I can vouch for the hamburgers at my favourite café-bar."

"Okay."

I parked the car, and we strolled the few hundred metres to the café taking a seat at a table outside on the walkway. Within minutes, the waitress appeared carrying a couple of menus and a bottle of water.

I ordered two hamburgers in my best Spanglish.

"I didn't know you could speak Spanish," Diane said.

I laughed. "I can't. Not really. Giles was fluent and so it made me lazy. Anything I know I learned after he died."

"It sounded pretty impressive to me, and the waitress understood."

"Only because I pointed to the picture of the hamburger as I said it."

Diane appeared distracted suddenly, so I followed her gaze to a young Spanish boy standing at the side of the café building smoking a cigarette. He was dressed in black trousers and a white shirt with an apron over the top. He was handsome in a long-haired, cool kind of way.

"There you go. Someone your age."

Her face flushed, but her eyes twinkled prettily.

AFTER LUNCH, we darted around the supermarket grabbing essentials. Neither of us could think about food after putting away the divine hamburgers with caramelised onions. Then we headed back to the villa.

"Help me make the beds, and then we can have a siesta," I said.

"I am a bit tired, actually."

"It's the heat. When in Rome as they say?"

"Are we in Rome?"

"No, silly. It's a saying—when in Rome, do as the Romans do. Meaning follow the customs of the locals."

"Ah, I get you."

We put the groceries away, made the beds, and then went our separate ways for a siesta.

It felt so good to be home.

THE NEXT FEW days came and went with us both unwinding. We strolled along the beach, read books, played cards and listened to music.

We'd had several texts from Ryan telling us Robert was still in a coma, and that he'd taken me up on my offer to stay at the house. I wondered what was going on with him and his ex. Just a healthy interest, I told myself.

On the third day, we strolled to the other end of the beach and into the back of the village for lunch.

"Shall we try something different today?" I suggested. "I'm sure you'll love tapas."

"At the same café?"

I grinned. "Are you hoping to see someone in particular there?"

"No!" she said, a little too quickly.

I wiggled my eyebrows at her. "If you say so."

We headed for the same table on the street, and the waitress was out before we'd even sat down.

We ordered a selection of tapas.

Diane kept gazing over to the café entrance.

"We could ask Angel if she knows of any youth clubs in the area."

"Youth clubs?"

"Well, I don't know what they call them nowadays, but there must be somewhere the kids hang about around here."

Diane gasped. She was eyeballing something behind me.

I turned to see the young waiter from the other day heading towards us carrying our order.

"Hola," he said, smiling broadly at Diane.

"Hi," she replied, shyly.

"This is my niece, Diane," I said.

"Diane. I am Samuel." He spoke slowly and carefully.

"You speak English?" I asked.

"Little." He smiled again at Diane before heading back inside.

"I think you've pulled," I said.

"Aunt Susie!" she squeaked, looking around to see if anybody overheard.

"Relax, I'm joking. He does seem to like you though. Anyway, tuck in. This dish is meatballs; that one potato. The pot dish is chorizo, which is a spicy sausage, and last but not least, frittata."

After lunch, I went inside to use the bathroom. When I returned, Samuel was bashfully chatting to Diane. I quickly stepped back inside to give them a few more minutes.

Samuel passed me, clearly pleased with himself.

"So?" I asked, approaching the table.

"He asked me to meet him later."

"Did he now? Gosh, he didn't waste much time."

"Not like that. He said he was meeting a few friends after work."

"Nice. What time?"

"That's the problem. I didn't understand him."

"What did he say?"

She shrugged. "De la tarde."

"That means in the evening, I think. What else did he say?"

"To meet on the beach. Something de la tarde."

"Cuatro? Cinco? Seis? Siete?"

"Seis. Yes, he said seis de la tarde."

"Okay, that means six pm. Flipping heck, Diane. I think we could both do with having Spanish lessons. What do you think?"

CHAPTER 42

"What will you wear?" I asked, as we strolled back along the beach.

"Maybe jeans. I only have one dress and this pair of shorts." She pulled at the black cotton shorts she was wearing.

"Bugger! I wanted to take you into town to buy some more dresses. You're welcome to look through my wardrobe and see if there's anything you like. We're not too different size-wise, and I'm always buying things I never wear."

"Okay."

That floored me. The Diane I met just a few weeks ago would've told me to eff-off if I'd suggested she wore my clothes.

Diane had a shower and got ready to go out. She chose a lightweight white blouse of mine with her jeans. She looked stunning.

"Shall I drop you off?" I asked.

"No, I'll be fine. I just have to walk along the beach. I'll be there in five minutes."

"Well, should I walk with you then?"

"No. Honestly, I'll be fine."

I had no doubt she'd be fine. Nothing untoward ever happened in our sleepy village.

I watched from the veranda as she walked off along the beach. She turned and waved several times until she was out of sight. Then I picked up the phone.

"Hi, Angel," I said. "Fancy a glass of wine?"

I BROUGHT Angel up to speed on everything.

"Where is Diane now?"

"She's meeting a local lad. The waiter from the village cafe."

"Samuel?"

"Yes. Do you know him?"

"He's a nice boy. I know his mother."

"Oh, good. I've been a little worried about her. She's been through such a lot."

"She'll be fine. Samuel is studying law and works at the café on his days off."

I made us a smoked chicken salad and opened a second bottle of wine. "I hope Diane doesn't need me to pick her up. I'll be too far gone." I laughed.

As we sat on the veranda watching the sun go down, we put the world to rights.

"I should be off. Marvin will be wondering where I am. It's nine o'clock." Angel got to her feet.

I walked her through the villa to the front door and waited until she reached her own villa across the road. I switched on the outside light, hoping Diane would come the road way now—it would be far too dark on the beach.

I filled the kettle and made myself a strong coffee. The wine had made me feel squiffy. Then I curled up on the sofa with my laptop.

A light tapping at the front door had me on my feet a few minutes later. It was Diane on the doorstep.

"Oh, thank goodness I got the right house," she gushed. "Everywhere looks different in the dark."

"I was beginning to worry. Is everything okay?"

"Better than okay. I've had a really good time. Samuel's lovely, and I met a few of his friends who don't speak much English, but we all managed to understand each other, I think."

"The best way to learn a language is to be shoved into the deep end, like this. You'll be fluent in a couple of months."

She laughed and plonked herself down on the sofa. "I doubt it, but Samuel tried to teach me a few phrases. Although I've forgotten them already." Her eyes sparkled when she spoke his name.

The tinkling of a text message sounded from my handbag. I reached for it, a feeling of dread at my core. I read the message. "It's Ryan. He said the hospital called. Robert's awake."

"Really?" she gasped. "Is he going to be alright?"

"I don't know, sweetie. But it's got to be a good sign, doesn't it?"

"I guess so. Let's hope he can tell the Detective who attacked him."

"Fingers crossed." I replied to Ryan then placed my phone on the coffee table. "Right, can I make you a hot drink before bed? I'm getting a bit tired. Did you eat anything while you were out?"

"Yes. We had onion rings."

"Are you sure they were onion rings?"

She nodded. "I think so. They looked like onion rings. What else could they have been?"

"I've a feeling they would be squid rings rather than onion rings, but I could be mistaken."

She made a gagging sound.

"What difference does it make? If you ate them, you must've liked them."

"Just the thought of squid makes me want to chuck up."

"Gosh, you're funny. How about a hot chocolate?"

"No, thanks. I'll just grab a glass of water and then I'll go to bed."

CHAPTER 43

They thought they could up and leave the country and they'd be safe. Well, they were in for a shock—they wouldn't get rid of me that easily.

I strolled around the villa, slumped down on the sofa, and picked up the phone off the table in front of me. It proved interesting reading. That prick from the bar had been messaging every day, but it was the last text that interested me. Retard Robert was awake and squealing like a little pig, no doubt.

I strolled through to the kitchen and dropped the phone onto the marble flooring. I stomped on the screen to be certain it was definitely smashed before kicking it underneath the cooker.

I then crept towards the bedroom.

Diane's piercing screams had me out of bed and across the landing in a flash. My raging heartbeat thundered in my ears.

I found her seated upright in her bed; her back tight against the wall, her arms covering her head.

"Hey! Hey! Come on, sweetie. It's just a dream. You're okay."

"He was here. He was here again."

"No, no, no. You're mistaken. We're in Spain. Nobody even knows where we are. It was a nightmare! You were dreaming."

"Check the windows and doors. I'm sure he was here. I heard him and I could smell him."

"Calm down. I'll check, I promise. But I can assure you nobody knows we're here."

Once she'd calmed down, I went to check the windows and doors as promised. Everywhere was securely locked. Then I returned to Diane's room and slid into bed beside her. "Try to get some sleep, sweetie. I'll stay right here."

I lay awake until I knew she was asleep. The backward step concerned me. She'd seemed so happy tonight after her date that I'd allowed myself to believe she was on the mend.

WHEN I WOKE the next morning, I was surprised Diane wasn't there. Padding through to the lounge, I found her curled on the sofa fast asleep. My heart swelled in my chest as I gazed down at her sleeping childlike face for a few minutes. Then I headed to the kitchen to make a pot of coffee.

Diane joined me out on the veranda a short while later.

"Good morning. How are you feeling?"

She scratched her head. "Confused. How did I make it onto the sofa?"

"I dunno. I presumed I must've been snoring, and you took off."

"No. The last thing I remember is you getting in bed with me."

"Really? That's strange. You must've sleep-walked."

She sat opposite me on the matching cane chair.

"Do you fancy a glass of orange juice?" I asked.

"You stay there. I'll get it. Can I get you one?"

"No, thanks. I'll stick with something a little stronger." I grinned and held up my steaming coffee mug.

"Sorry to wake you again. The feeling seemed so real last night, but I feel embarrassed now." She headed inside.

"Don't be silly," I called after her. "I've found lots of things seem far worse in the middle of the night."

She reappeared with a glass of juice and returned to her seat. "Does it happen to you too?"

I nodded. "I'd say it happens to most people. If there's something playing on your mind, it's ten times worse in the small hours. Shall we go for a walk? Maybe a paddle in the sea? It's going to be a scorcher today."

"Yeah, I'd like that. And I'm meeting Samuel again later."

"Ooh! Andre's been well and truly dumped then, I take it?"

She shrugged, a coy smile playing around the corners of her mouth. "Andre who?"

"That's my girl. Onwards and upwards is my motto."

"Is that what you're doing with Ryan?"

"Fat chance of that. Especially if we're staying here. Nice thought, but too much baggage and not much point."

"Shame though. He's nice, and he obviously fancies you."

"Hey, cheeky."

"What? It's true."

"Whatever." I drained my cup wanting to avoid a full-on discussion about my love life. "Right, I'll go and get ready."

I padded through to my bedroom and threw on a light cotton sundress. Then I headed to the lounge for my bag and phone. My phone wasn't on the coffee table where I'd left it.

Diane appeared in the doorway. "What's wrong?"

"Oh, nothing. I've misplaced my phone, that's all." I smiled at her, not wanting to freak her out after her nightmare last night.

"You want to use mine?"

"No, it's okay. It'll turn up. You ready to go?"

We both walked barefoot down the rocks and onto the beach.

The air was still and I could tell it was going to be a scorcher.

Instead of heading along the beach as usual, we both headed straight for the water. I had a fear of swimming in the sea, but I loved to paddle up to my knees. I'd even been known to sit in the shallows on the stifling hot days.

Diane paddled out a little further than me. I heard her phone ringing. She fished it from her dress pocket and, as if in slow motion, I watched it topple from her fingers and plop into the sea. She clamped her hands to her mouth and stared at me in total shock.

After a moment of silence, we both burst into hysterics.

"Oops," she said after a few minutes, causing another bout of laughter. Then she suddenly went serious. "I've lost all my contacts again."

"It's okay. You can contact everybody on Facebook. I'll buy you a new phone next time we go into town."

We spent an hour splashing in the sea. Then, once we'd worked up an appetite, we strolled back to the villa arm in arm.

AFTER BREAKFAST, I did another sweep of the place looking for my phone—it was nowhere to be found. I left Diane waiting to hear it ring and crossed the driveway to ask Angel to call my number. It went straight to voicemail.

"When did you last have it?" Angel asked.

"Last night, after you left. We got a text telling us Robert had woken from his coma. Then I left it on the coffee table, but it was gone by this morning."

"That's strange."

"I know. But I don't want to freak Diane out. She had a nightmare last night. She thought the killer was here."

"Here?" Angel shuddered dramatically.

"It was just a nightmare. I thought she'd left that fear in the UK, but I was mistaken."

"If your phone has been stolen, and she thought somebody was in the property, maybe she was right?"

I laughed. "Remind me not to let Diane hear your theory. She'll be on the next flight out of here."

Angel winced and then made a lip zipping motion.

Angel's words unsettled me, and my brain began to chatter. Could there be any truth in the old lady's mutterings? A chill ran up my spine. The hairs on my arms bristled. What if Andre had told the killer where we were?

CHAPTER 44

Ryan tried calling Susanna's number for the fifth time that morning and let out an exasperated sigh when it went straight to voicemail.

He didn't know if she'd got his message about Robert. He wished he'd asked for a landline number or email address or something. He didn't even know if young Diane had a phone with her and no way of finding her number if she had.

Still staying at their house, he found an address book in the top drawer of the office desk. But when he dialled the number entry for Diane he was greeted with a disconnected tone.

"Bloody hell. What is it with people and mobile phones?" he muttered.

After taking a shower, he dressed in trousers and shirt and headed off to the hotel. He'd stayed away for a few days, but Fiona had called him with the updated roster and she'd made him promise to turn up.

Although tempted to leave her in the lurch, he couldn't do that to the staff or the guests. He would go in on his rostered days until he made his decision on what to do. He knew he couldn't drag his heels. Susanna didn't mind him staying while they were in Spain, but he was pretty certain her hospitality wouldn't extend beyond that.

AFTER A LONG LEISURELY LUNCH, Diane and I strolled into the village to the only little clothes shop. They only sold sun dresses and novelty t-shirts. Diane had fallen in love with a dress she'd seen in the window last night, and she wanted to wear it to impress Samuel later.

"One size fits all," she grumbled as she glanced at the label.

"Isn't that a good thing? At least it will definitely fit you."

"I just don't know how they can say something will fit everyone. Look at that woman over there." She nodded at a voluptuous woman eating an ice-cream. "How could something fit me and her?"

I shrugged, stifling a grin. "Go and try it on."

She waved at the assistant and moments later emerged from the changing room wearing the flowing white cheesecloth dress that had red, poppy-like flowers printed all over it. She looked stunning.

"Oh, wow! I must say, I'm loving this new un-goth look."

"Un-goth? Is that even a real word?"

"Possibly not. But you know what I mean."

She swished the dress and admired her reflection in the mirror. "I'm tired of wearing black. Bright colours make my mood lighter if that makes sense?"

"Perfect sense. Now go and take it off, before you twirl a hole in the carpet."

In the time it took for her to change back into her own clothes, I'd paid for the dress and was standing out on the street waiting for her.

We strolled back to the villa along the beach and were both parched when we arrived home.

"What time are you meeting Samuel?" I asked.

"He's working until eight and I said I'd meet him at the end of the beach just after that. I hope his plans haven't changed though, now I don't have a phone."

"You could always call him at the restaurant."

"Nah, it should be fine. What will you do tonight? I feel a little mean leaving you alone two nights in a row."

"Oh, don't you worry about me. I'll be fine. I might even ask Angel if I can have a soak in her Jacuzzi bathtub. She always offers, and I really fancy a lazy pamper night."

"Eew, won't you feel funny with her weirdo husband there?"

I snorted. "Marvin's not a bit weird. He's lovely."

"I think he's weird. It's the way he stares and doesn't say a word."

"Because he can't speak English, that's all. I've heard him chatter away to Angel when it suits him."

"Well, I don't like him. He gives me the creeps."

Sitting on the veranda as the sun began to set, I watched Diane walk back along the beach, her sandals in her hand. The fine cheesecloth fabric flowed behind her prettily in the light breeze.

I finished my crossword puzzle, grabbed my toiletry bag and towel, before heading over to Angel's house.

She saw me coming from the kitchen window and opened the door for me before I got there.

"Are you sure it's okay, Angel?" I asked.

"Of course, it is. Marvin and I still use it though we're worried we might not get out of it one day." She chuckled.

"And Marvin doesn't mind?"

"I told you. It's fine—he's even cleaned all the pipes for you." She handed me a glass of wine before leading me to her large terracotta-tiled bathroom. "Take as long as you like. We're out the back when you've had enough."

I ran the steaming hot water and stepped out of my light cotton slip, feeling exhausted for some reason. Lying chin-deep in the water a few minutes later, I hit the Jacuzzi button and the low rumble startled me as the bubbles appeared. I'd had every intention of reading, but I felt my heavy eyes close. I just gave in to the drifting sensation.

CHAPTER 45

The sound of police sirens woke me from a deep sleep. I had no idea how long I'd actually been lying in the glorious bubbles. A rapid knocking at the bathroom door caused me to sit upright and sent a torrent of water cascading over the sides of the tub.

"Yes? It's open." I glanced down to ensure I was fully covered in case it was Marvin.

The door flung open and Angel rushed in. "Sorry, Susie. But something's happened in the village. I thought you'd want to know with Diane heading that way."

I shot out of the water no longer bothered who saw me in the buff. I just needed to check Diane was alright. After throwing on my dress, I rushed out to the street.

The sound of sirens was unusual in this little village. In fact, I can't ever remember hearing it in all the years we'd been holidaying in the area.

"What do you think it is?" I asked as Angel caught up with me.

"I've no idea. But it's something bad."

Marvin appeared, carrying his garden trowel. He spoke to Angel as he began tending the potted plants under an outdoor light.

They glanced in the direction of the village centre.

"Maybe you should call Diane," Angel said.

"I can't. She dropped her phone in the sea this morning."

"Oh, of course. I forgot."

"I need to go and find out what's happening. She might not be home for hours yet and I'll be stressing all night. What time is it anyway?"

"Almost nine. I'll come too. We can take my car. Marvin can stay here in case she comes back before us."

We didn't get very far in the car. The traffic was backed up—it didn't seem to be moving at all.

Angel parked and we left on foot. We were half running, half walking—desperate to find out what had happened.

We came across a group of people huddled together.

"What's happened?"

They all looked at me as though I'd grown an extra head.

Angel spoke in Spanish. "Alguien encontró un cadáver," they all responded at the same time.

Although not fluent in Spanish, I knew what the word *cadaver* meant—a dead body. I didn't hang around to hear any more. I took off at a run. Blind panic was causing me to hyperventilate. I needed to calm down before I passed out.

As I neared the far edge of the village, a uniformed police officer blocked my way.

"Please, I need to find my niece," I cried, trying to scramble past him.

He shoved me and yelled something I couldn't understand. I knew not to mess with him.

Angel appeared at my side and tore a strip off the officer. At least he had the good grace to appear embarrassed. He told her something, but I couldn't decipher any of it.

"What did he say?" I asked.

She shrugged me off and rattled off another long speech to him.

The officer shrugged and then nodded.

"What? What's happened?"

"A young couple have been found at the entrance to the beach—their heads smashed in. They're both dead."

"No!" I cried, dropping to my knees. "It can't be her."

"He confirmed it was Samuel and a young woman. Not a local. I'm sorry, Susie, but it sounds like it might be Diane."

CHAPTER 46

I approached the villa from the beach and washed my bloody hands at the outside tap. I was livid. How dare he snog her face off like that? I hadn't meant to kill them, but seeing them like that had made me wild.

I peered through the window checking the villa was empty before entering. I needed a few items, and then I intended to lie low for a while. There was no chance of escape while the entire village was out on the street.

"Quién está ahí?"

I froze at the deep, gruff voice right behind me.

The world sped on around me, but I couldn't grasp much of what was going on. Angel took control, jabbering away in Spanish, giving them all what for.

A senior officer appeared and beckoned for me to follow him. He led us to a quieter place behind the police cordon, and he began speaking to Angel saying the odd word here and there in English.

"He wants to know if you have a photograph of Diane?"

I shook my head. "I don't have any at all. I had some on my phone but that's gone missing."

She translated for the cop, who replied, wrote something on a notepad, and then abruptly left.

"What did he say?"

"That you will need to identify the body after it's been taken to the morgue."

"I need to see her now." I turned and began to chase after the officer. "Hey! Come back here."

Angel grabbed me by the arm. "He has my number, Susie. Let's go home. Maybe Diane's there already."

My stomach muscles clenched. She was right. Diane was probably waiting for me at home. I needed to believe it wasn't my beautiful niece lying dead at the entrance to the beach. Why would it be?

We pushed through the growing crowd and almost ran to the car.

All my senses were on overdrive. I felt aware of every bump in the road. The noise from the indicator was so loud, and the two minute journey seemed to go on forever.

I could tell Diane wasn't home as soon as we pulled up outside. The villa was in darkness. But I still ran inside calling her name, anyway.

Nothing.

Angel appeared in the doorway as I returned to the front of the villa. "Anything?"

"No sign of her."

"Marvin isn't here, is he?"

"Nobody's here. Isn't he at home?"

She shook her head. "The front door was wide open but there's no sign of him."

I knew how fastidious Marvin was about locking everywhere

up. "That's odd. Maybe he found Diane, and they've gone to look for us?"

Angel nodded. "Of course. That will be it."

"Can't you call him?"

"When have you even seen Marvin with a phone?"

"Sorry, I'm not thinking straight."

Angel rubbed my shoulder. "Shall I make us a hot drink?"

"I could do with something a little stronger, to be honest."

"I have a bottle of brandy from Christmas. Should I go and get it?"

I smiled and nodded. "Thanks, Angel." Standing at the window, I stared out to the street praying Diane and Marvin would just appear. But I didn't believe they would—Diane wouldn't be coming home again.

CHAPTER 47

The brandy took the edge off my nerves, but when neither Marvin nor Diane had arrived an hour later Angel began pacing the floor.

"Something terrible must've happened. Marvin never goes anywhere on foot, and we had the car."

I couldn't find the strength to comfort her. Instead I watched on, emotionless, as tears filled her eyes. Pouring two more brandies, I handed a glass to her.

She stopped pacing and swallowed it down. Wincing, she placed a hand on her chest while she dealt with the initial sensations of the fiery liquid.

"I need to call the police to report Marvin missing," Angel said, from the opposite end of the sofa.

I nodded my agreement, still numb to everything, in my shocked state.

"I don't understand where he could've got to. It just doesn't make sense."

I wanted to scream at her to shut up! I couldn't cope with all her jabber. At least Marvin was big enough and ugly enough to take care of himself. Diane was just a girl. She looked like a young woman but she still had a lot of growing up to do. I only prayed she would get that chance.

ANGEL RANG the policeman from earlier.

By the sounds of things, his first instinct was Marvin could be a suspect—that was until Angel confirmed he'd been with her the entire time.

Lights lit up the front of the villa a few moments later, and we both almost fell over each other to get to the door first.

A junior officer stood on the doorstep. Once again, the language barrier caused me a problem.

"He's come to take our statements," Angel said.

"I don't know how he intends to do that if he doesn't speak English."

She conveyed my concerns to the officer who gave an animated response.

"It's just a formality at this stage," Angel said. "He wants to see Diane's bedroom, and is asking for a photograph of her."

"I don't have a photograph," I snapped. "I told the other cop earlier."

"You have her passport, I presume?" Angel patted my hand.

I nodded and led the officer to Diane's bedroom. "Tell him I don't know what he's looking for, but this has only been Diane's bedroom for a few days."

The officer shrugged when Angel told him what I'd said.

I found Diane's passport in the bedside cabinet and handed it to the officer. "Is this the girl you found?" I asked.

He shook his head as he responded.

"Did he say no?" I gasped.

"He said he doesn't know. He hasn't seen the body."

"For God's sake! How long is this going to go on for? What if it's not Diane but some other poor girl? That means my niece is still out there, maybe in trouble. We need to find out if it's her or not."

Once the cop left, Angel and I settled on the sofa. Neither of us spoke a word, caught up in our own thoughts.

I don't know how long we stayed like that, but when I glanced around I noticed Angel was asleep.

I envied her knowing from experience that sleep would evade me.

I got to my feet and crept to the back door. I needed some fresh air.

The light from the porch lit my way down the craggy rocks to the sand. I had to rely on the pale light from the half-moon.

I walked from instinct and memory rather than sight. Strolling along, my gaze focused on the distant lights at the opposite end of the beach.

A strange grunting sound infiltrated my chattering mind. What the hell was it?

I walked quickly since the sound appeared to be getting louder, and I could make out a dark shape on the sand.

My heart stopped.

The flowing delicate fabric blowing in the breeze was undoubtedly Diane's new dress.

"Diane?" I screamed and ran towards the mound. I stumbled on something and collapsed onto the wet sand.

The moon peeked from behind a cloud and illuminated the body of the person lying face down beside me.

"Oh, my God, Diane. Can you hear me? Are you okay?" I cried, rolling her onto her back.

CHAPTER 48

I didn't waste any time. Diane was exhausted as far as I could tell, but very much alive.

As though suddenly superhuman, I dragged her along the beach and carried her up the rocks, screaming for Angel the entire way.

Angel suddenly appeared at the doorway, in a total kerfuffle. "What is it? What's happened?"

"Quick, help me get her inside."

Between us, we bundled Diane in through the kitchen and onto the sofa.

"Is she injured?" Angel asked, wiping the sand from Diane's arms and legs.

"I don't think so." Shaking profusely, I forced myself to calm down and take stock of the situation. "I think she's in shock. She went like this after her parents were killed."

"Diane? Can you hear me, dear?" Angel wiped the straggly hair from the girl's face.

"Will you phone the police, Angel? Tell them the dead girl isn't Diane." I knew there was no point trying myself, especially in my heightened state. And any Spanish I knew this morning had suddenly left me.

Angel pulled her phone from her pocket and moved to the front of the house to make the call.

I squatted down beside Diane and checked her pulse and lifted each of her eyelids. Not that I knew what I was looking for. I had to do something—I felt so helpless.

"The police said they'll be back to interview us and Diane as soon as they get the chance. But do you think we need to take her to the hospital?"

I shook my head. "I'm hoping she'll come around soon. I can't tell you how relieved I am—although some other poor family will be faced with devastating news by morning."

Angel looked away, and I realised she was blinking back tears.

"Oh, I'm sorry, Angel. I didn't think. Marvin will be home soon, you'll see."

She nodded, patting me on my arm and forcing a smile onto her face. "Oh, don't mind me, love. I'm being a silly old sod." Her cockney accent sounded stronger when she was worried.

I pushed myself to my feet and went to hug Angel.

"What's that on your hands?" Angel's face screwed up. "Is it blood?"

Startled, I looked down. I was shocked at the sight of my bloodstained hands. I returned to Diane's side and patted down her dress. "She must've been stabbed or something." I pulled apart the buttons of her dress trying to find the source of the bleeding.

Suddenly, Diane woke and batted my hands away. She scrambled backwards on the sofa. "Leave me alone!" she screamed.

CHAPTER 49

"Hey, hey, hey!" I cried, reaching for Diane's flailing hands. "You're okay, sweetheart. You're home and safe now."

Pushing herself back as far as she could go, she ended up clambering to her feet, on top of the sofa, screaming hysterically.

Angel and I both spoke in soft, soothing voices and tried to calm Diane down. A few minutes later, her screams turned to sobs, and she slumped back down on the sofa.

"Can you tell us what happened, sweetie?" I sat beside her and stroked her brow.

She stared at me as though seeing me for the first time—eyes brimming with tears.

"Did you see Marvin, dear?" Angel said softly.

Diane gasped, clearly startled we weren't alone.

"Don't worry. It's only Angel. You're safe," I said, shaking my head at Angel. "But the police will want to talk to you, darling. They'll be here soon."

Diane pushed my hand away and glared at me, her lips pulled back from her teeth in a snarl. "Get your fucking hands off me."

Completely taken aback, I staggered to my feet.

"Hey, hey. There's no need to speak to me like that. We only want to help you."

"I don't need your help," she growled. "I trusted you. You told me I was safe here."

I gulped down a huge lump that had suddenly formed in my throat. "You *are* safe here. There's no reason to think this has anything to do with what happened in England."

"Wake up!" she yelled. "I told you he was here last night, and now this has happened. Samuel and that slut may have deserved everything that happened to them, but Marvin didn't. He's never hurt a soul in his life."

I couldn't speak. Couldn't move a muscle. What the hell was she talking about?

"What do you mean? What happened to Marvin?" Angel's eyes were wide with disbelief.

"What happened to Marvin?" Diane mimicked.

"Why are you being like this?" I was completely confused. "And whose blood are you covered in?"

Diane's face cracked into a manic smile. "Whose do you think?"

CHAPTER 50

Ryan placed the pint of Guinness on the bar.

"Thanks, mate. Don't tell your missus, but she doesn't pull a pint as well as you do," said Nik Plumley, the local dentist.

"She's not my missus anymore, Nik, and I have no intention of sparing her feelings."

"She's still your wife. Surely she'll see she's better off with you than that deadbeat she's knocking around with."

"I don't care if she does, to be honest, mate. She's made her bed, and she can lie in it. I couldn't see it at first, but she's actually done me a favour."

"You're not planning on scarpering, are you?"

"Who knows, mate? I'm a free agent right now, and I intend to go wherever the wind takes me."

"Well, there are worse positions to be in, I suppose. In fact, I'm a little jealous. The thought of poking around in people's cavities for the next twenty years doesn't fill me with joy."

Ryan shuddered. "I don't know how you do it, mate. You've got a stronger constitution than me."

The door swung open and Conrad entered.

"Hey, me old mucka, how's it going?" Ryan asked, wiping his

cloth along the bar as he approached the mithered-looking Detective.

"Not so good, to be honest, Ryan. Can you spare me a minute?" He nodded over to the far booth.

"Give me a sec, and I'll get someone to mind the bar." Ryan popped his head through the adjoining door of the hotel and called Bernice, the new receptionist, who, from the expression on her face, thought she was above pulling pints. "It's only for a few minutes. It's not as if we're even busy, so just do it. Just because my wife employed you, doesn't mean you don't need to listen to me. I'm the one paying your wages, you know."

Conrad raised his eyebrows when Ryan walked out from behind the bar. "Bit harsh?"

"You heard that?"

Conrad nodded, a smirk on his face. "We all did."

"Well, she pisses me off. You'd think I just asked her to pick up dog shit with her bare hands. Anyway, what can I do for you? You seem stressed."

"I was hoping you'd know where I can find Susanna and her niece? I've been calling since yesterday and the calls keep going through to voicemail."

"Didn't they tell you? They've gone to Spain for a while. Diane was freaked out after her uncle was attacked. Can't say I blame her to be honest." The expression on Conrad's face made Ryan stop talking. "What is it?"

"Robert's made a statement."

"You mean he knows who clobbered him?"

Conrad nodded, his mouth set in a firm line as he inhaled deeply.

CHAPTER 51

I stared at Angel as the hair on my neck shot upright. "This isn't a joke, Diane. Tell me—whose blood is it?"

The sneer remained as she turned to face Angel defiantly. "He may only speak in Spanish, but his screams could be understood in any language."

I gasped, reaching out for Angel's arm. It took a few moments for Diane's words to sink in.

"What have you done to my Marvin, you twisted bitch?" Angel screamed, launching herself at Diane.

Diane was up on her feet in a flash and she kicked the old woman in the throat, sending her flying backwards to crash in a clattering heap onto the glass coffee table.

"Get the fuck off me, you stupid bitch!" Diane's voice had taken on a strange timbre.

I screamed and dropped beside Angel, who had a deep gash in her forearm. "What the hell's got into you, Diane? She's an old woman."

"An interfering old bag, more like."

I ignored my deranged niece, focusing instead on the blood pumping from Angel's arm. I grabbed the fleecy pink blanket from the arm of the chair and held it to the gash. "We need an ambulance. I think you might've nicked an artery."

I reached for Angel's phone which now sat amongst shards of glass in the middle of the floor.

Diane threw herself at me, knocking me off my feet, and slammed me down beside Angel. "No ambulance," she roared.

"But she's going to bleed to death if we don't get some help," I cried, totally shocked at the force behind Diane's assault.

She turned and walked back to the sofa, her right leg dragging as she went.

"Diane? What's happened to you?"

She smiled, a sneaky, conspiratorial smile. "Diane's a fucking weakling. She didn't deserve to live over me."

"What are you talking about?" I asked, shaking my head in confusion.

That sly smile once again.

"What did you do to Marvin?"

Angel's eyes had closed, as she held onto the blanket. Now they sprang open, staring at Diane.

"I told him to back off, but he wouldn't listen. I only wanted to come back to change out of this fucking dress, but he couldn't keep his nose out of it."

"So what did you do to him, Diane?"

"I already told you—I'm not Diane, *Auntie Suze*."

"Who the hell are you, then?" It suddenly dawned on me. The way she said my name—the raspy voice, the limp, it all made sense. "Dylan?"

"Give the lady a cigar."

"Why? Was it you all along?"

"That control freak father of ours didn't want us to enjoy ourselves; always nagging. Diane didn't mind. But the more she tried to appease him, the stricter he became."

"So you just killed him? And murdered my lovely sister too? You're sick!"

As we spoke, I slowly turned, positioning myself between her and the door. Angel was now unconscious from losing so much blood, and I needed to get out and get some help quickly.

"I told you—I'm not Diane."

"You *are* Diane. Dylan didn't live more than an hour."

"You don't know what you're talking about. I was here all along. It's Diane who's gone. I was willing to live with her, but she kept fighting me. The fucking do-gooder."

"What happened tonight? What caused all this?" I pointed at Angel.

"Samuel tried to call. To cancel the date, but because Diane dropped her phone into the sea, he didn't get hold of her. When we got there, he had some other slag on his arm."

"So what did you do?" I cried knowing exactly what she'd done but not wanting to believe it.

"Diane couldn't cope, so I had to take over. I waited until the cheating prick led his new girl to the exact same spot he'd taken Diane last night, and then I smashed their fucking heads right in."

CHAPTER 52

"Diane? You've got to be kidding me." Ryan jumped to his feet and began pacing the floor beside the booth. "Are you sure he's not mistaken? He might be brain damaged and hallucinating."

"He's as shocked as we are, Ryan. He described it in minute detail. He said she had a crazed look in her eyes and extraordinary strength. Now I guess he had to say that—being knocked into the middle of next week by a young girl isn't anything to boast about, but the rest of what he said I believe."

"But you saw her. She was terrified. That couldn't have been an act."

Conrad shrugged. "Who can tell these days? I thought I'd seen everything there was to see, but this has floored me to be honest. Do you have any way of getting hold of Susanna?"

"No! I've been trying for a couple of days. Both numbers are going to voicemail. What should we do?"

"She didn't give you an address? Any information at all?"

"South of Spain. The main city is Malaga if I remember rightly. She said it was a small village on the coast. Fuck! I wish I'd paid more attention now."

"I'll do some more digging. Someone must know their whereabouts."

"Maybe Robert can help. Or Diane's boyfriend. Let me know, please, Conrad. I won't settle till I know she's safe."

"Will do, buddy."

Ryan turned back to the bar once Conrad had left.

Bernice gave him a dirty look as he approached her.

"Any chance you can paste a smile on your face? It looks like a smacked arse. If not, piss off home. I'm not in the mood for your shit today."

She made as though to respond and then changed her mind.

"I'm off out. Mind the bar until I get back." He grabbed his keys and jacket and took off without a backwards glance.

CHAPTER 53

"Let me call an ambulance for Angel. She's lost a lot of blood," I pleaded.

Diane twiddled Angel's phone between her finger and thumb, a sickly-sweet grin on her face.

I couldn't believe what was happening. My dear, sweet niece was a monster. How had nobody suspected her? Robert had tried telling me, but I'd refused to listen to him.

"Why are you doing this, Diane?"

"I told you. I'm Dylan. Diane is a wuss."

Now closer to the backdoor, I made a dart for it—desperate to get some help for Angel more than anything.

Diane was much faster than I gave her credit for and slammed me into the kitchen wall. "Do you think I'm fucking stupid?" she yelled, grabbing a carving knife from the block on the benchtop. She yanked me back by my hair and dragged me onto the balcony.

"The police will be here soon," I cried. "Don't make it any harder on yourself."

"Shut the fuck up, *Auntie* Suze," she laughed and threw me to the marble flooring raising the knife over my head.

"What the hell happened to cause you to be so cruel and heartless?"

"You think this is cruel and heartless? You ain't seen nothing yet." She lurched forward and plunged the knife into my shoulder.

White hot pain shot through me, and, in disbelief I looked down at the knife handle protruding from me. I knew, considering the length of the blade and the depth of my body, the knife had gone straight through me.

She put her foot on my other shoulder, grabbed the handle, and kicked me backwards. The blade came away in one excruciating motion.

I screamed and flinched expecting Diane to go again, but she didn't. After a few minutes, I forced myself to look up and see what she was doing.

"You must be impressed. All those cops and that stupid fucking Detective on the case, and not one of them suspected me."

"But I saw the state of you. And somebody broke into the office like you said. The door was kicked in." No matter what my eyes and mind told me, my heart refused to believe my sister's daughter was a cold-blooded killer.

"You stupid bitch. It was Dad hiding in the office like the coward he was. We fought, and I grabbed a knife and he ran. Didn't get too far though. I wanted him to go upstairs, to waste him and Mum together but he began having a fit or heart attack or something, so I had no choice but to kill him on the stairs."

"But you weren't covered in blood. The police would've known."

"I'd already removed my clothing. Then I had a shower and got dressed again."

"You said you saw someone standing over your mother in the bedroom."

"That was me in the mirror. You were all so gullible."

I lifted my fingers that were clamped to my shoulder, and

blood oozed from the wound. Just then I heard the sound of a car pulling onto the drive at the front of the house.

"I still don't understand why?" I said, wanting to distract her for a moment longer.

"You've said yourself what a control freak Dad was. Mum was no better. But I knew they were leaving everything to me in their will."

"You won't get away with this, Diane. You'll be locked up in a secure unit for the rest of your life. *You're a fucking lunatic!*" I screamed the last words as someone knocked on the front door.

Diane raised the knife once more.

I curled into a ball and felt the blade glance off my skull and tear into the flesh of my cheek. I screamed again.

Moments later, the villa was filled with armed police.

Blood poured from my head and into my eyes making it hard to see. I wiped it off with my forearm.

Diane stood on the edge of the veranda. The strange grin had returned to her face.

Several yells came from inside as the police approached us, their firearms drawn. One of the officers began yelling at her in Spanish.

As Diane lifted the knife, the officer gave the signal to fire.

Instead of lunging once again for me, Diane slammed the blade into her own neck.

Shots rang out, and I watched as she toppled backwards, off the veranda, landing on the rocks below with a sickening thud.

EPILOGUE

I LOOKED AT MY REFLECTION IN THE MIRROR.

My right eye was closed—black and blue bruising surrounding it, and a long line of stitches graced the centre of my right cheek. The doctor had told me I was lucky. The blade had only given me superficial cuts to my head and had gouged a dent in my skull, but nothing serious.

Diane was dead by the time anyone reached her. I didn't know what had caused her death, whether the knife to her throat, the gunshots or the fall to the rocks below, but I couldn't help feeling relieved she hadn't survived. I couldn't bear the thought of her having to spend the rest of her life behind bars labelled a killer. I didn't know what had happened to cause my sweet niece to flip and commit those murders, but I was willing to believe Dylan and Diane were two very different people. I would've known otherwise.

"Knock, knock." Angel's voice from the doorway startled me.

"Oh, Angel," I cried, tears flooding my eyes in an instant. "How are you feeling? I was so worried about you, and I couldn't understand most of what the doctor and nurses were saying."

"You need to get back to your Spanish classes, my dear. I'm fine. A few stitches, but I'll be as good as new in a few weeks."

"And Marvin?"

Angel paused, inhaling deeply before replying. "They found him on the sand, partially buried but alive, thank God."

"Oh, poor Marvin. Is he going to be okay?"

"I think so. She'd used his own garden trowel on him and nearly finished the job too. You must've disturbed her."

"I heard a strange grunting sound when I found her. I should've looked."

"It wasn't your fault. How could you've known?" Angel said, kindly.

I shook my head not sure I would've been so understanding had the roles been reversed.

"Are you ready to go home? The doctor has discharged you."

"Really? Then yes, I'm more than ready to get out of here. Although I'm unsure where home is now."

"Come back with me for a while. I have a feeling we're going to need to support each other for now."

ANGEL and I returned to her house just stopping by my villa long enough for me to grab my overnight bag. Marvin would be in hospital for some time, but he was lucky to be alive. I still felt immense guilt for bringing Diane into their lives.

I contemplated leaving Spain altogether, but the police still needed to talk to me and tie up some loose ends, so I had no choice but to stay put for now.

Neither of us felt much like eating, but we went through the motions of making dinner sitting down at the table and then throwing all the food in the fridge for later. Then Angel excused herself and I heard her sobbing from her bedroom soon after.

I headed to the beach to give her some privacy.

The rocks below my veranda had been taped off, but I got as close as I could. Diane had been my only living relative, and, despite what she had done, I missed her terribly.

I saw a man strolling on the beach towards me. He seemed a little overdressed, in full length jeans, long-sleeved shirt and jacket, not to mention his boots. It wasn't until he was upon me that I recognized him. My heart caught in my throat.

"Ryan," I whispered, and staggered to my feet.

"You're a hard lady to find. You know that?"

I ran into his outstretched arms, needing his comfort more than anything in the world at that moment.

"How did you know?" I asked.

"Conrad told me and has kept me informed on and off the entire journey. I couldn't believe it and just needed to be here for you."

"What about the hotel?"

"Let them run it into the ground for all I care. I'm well rid of it and them."

"Really?"

"When I thought you were in danger, I was in no doubt as to where I needed to be. By your side. If you'll have me, that is." He looked a little unsure for a moment.

"I've always been a sucker for strays. You can stay with me for a while—until I know whether you're housetrained or not that is." I smiled, grateful I didn't have to face the next few days alone.

The End

ALSO BY NETTA NEWBOUND

BEHIND SHADOWS
Adam Stanley Thriller Series Book 1
NETTA NEWBOUND

Amanda Flynn's life is falling apart. Her spineless cheating husband has taken her beloved children. Her paedophile father, who went to prison vowing revenge, has been abruptly released. And now someone in the shadows is watching her every move.

When one by one her father and his cohorts turn up dead, Amanda finds herself at the centre of several murder investigations—with no alibi and a diagnosis of Multiple Personality Disorder. Abandoned, scared and fighting to clear her name as more and more damning evidence comes to light, Amanda begins to doubt her own sanity.

Could she really be a brutal killer?

A gripping psychological thriller not to be missed...

An Edge of your Seat Psychological Thriller Novel

For Melissa May, happily married to Gavin for the best part of thirty years, life couldn't get much better. Her world is ripped apart when she discovers Gavin is HIV positive. The shock of his duplicity and irresponsible behaviour re-awakens a psychiatric condition Melissa has battled since childhood. Fuelled by rage and a heightened sense of right and wrong, Melissa takes matters into her own hands.

Homicide detective Adam Stanley is investigating what appear to be several random murders. When evidence comes to light, linking the victims, the case seems cut and dried and an arrest is made. However, despite all the damning evidence, including a detailed confession, Adam is certain the killer is still out there. Now all he has to do is prove it.

MIND BENDER

Adam Stanley Thriller Series · Book 3

NETTA NEWBOUND

An Edge of your Seat Psychological Thriller Novel

Detective Inspector Adam Stanley returns to face his most challenging case yet. Someone is randomly killing ordinary Pinevale citizens. Each time DI Stanley gets close to the killer, the killer turns up dead—the next victim in someone's crazy game.

Meanwhile, his girlfriend's brother, Andrew, currently on remand for murder, escapes and kidnaps his own 11-year-old daughter. However, tragedy strikes, leaving the girl in grave danger.

Suffering a potentially fatal blow himself, how can DI Stanley possibly save anyone?

A Compelling Psychological Thriller Novel.

In this fast-moving suspense novel, Detective Adam Stanley searches for Miles Muldoon, a hardworking, career-minded businessman, and Pinevale's latest serial killer.

Evidence puts Muldoon at each scene giving the police a prima facie case against him.

But as the body count rises, and their suspect begins taunting them, this seemingly simple case develops into something far more personal when Muldoon turns his attention to Adam and his family.

Ghost Writer is a 24,000 word novella.

Bestselling thriller author Natalie Cooper has a crippling case of writer's block. With her deadline looming, she finds the only way she can write is by ditching her laptop and reverting back to pen and paper. But the story which flows from the pen is not just another work of fiction.

Unbeknown to her, a gang of powerful and deadly criminals will stop at nothing to prevent the book being written.

Will Natalie manage to finish the story and expose the truth before it's too late? Or could the only final chapter she faces be her own?

A Gripping and Incredibly Moving Psychological Suspense Novel

When Geraldine MacIntyre's marriage falls apart, she returns to her childhood home expecting her mother to welcome her with open arms. Instead, she finds all is not as it should be with her parents.

James Dunn, a successful private investigator and crime writer, is also back in his hometown, to help solve a recent spate of vicious rapes. He is thrilled to discover his ex-classmate, and love of his life, Geraldine, is back, minus the hubby, and sets out to get the girl. However, he isn't the only interested bachelor in the quaint, country village. Has he left it too late?

Embellished Deception is a thrilling, heart-wrenching and thought provoking story of love, loss and deceit.

An Edge of your Seat Psychological Thriller Novel

Geraldine and baby Grace arrive in Nottingham to begin their new life with author James Dunn.

Lee Barnes, James' best friend and neighbour, is awaiting the imminent release of his wife, Lydia, who has served six years for infanticide. But he's not as prepared as he thought. In a last ditch effort to make things as perfect as possible his already troubled life takes a nose dive.

Geraldine and James combine their wits to investigate several historical, unsolved murders for James' latest book. James is impressed by her keen eye and instincts. However, because of her inability to keep her mouth shut, Geri, once again, finds herself the target of a crazed and vengeful killer.

A Gripping Psychological Suspense Novel.

Geri and James return in their most explosive adventure to date.

When next door neighbour, Lydia, gives birth to her second healthy baby boy, James and Geri pray their friend can finally be happy and at peace. But, little do they know Lydia's troubles are far from over.

Meanwhile, Geri is researching several historic, unsolved murders for James' new book. She discovers one of the prime suspects now resides in Spring Pines Retirement Village, the scene of not one, but two recent killings.

Although the police reject the theory, Geri is convinced the cold case they're researching is linked to the recent murders. But how? Will she regret delving so deeply into the past?

THE BEST-SELLING SERIAL KILLER THRILLER THAT EVERYONE IS TALKING ABOUT

Life couldn't get much better for Hannah. She accepts her dream job in Manchester, and easily makes friends with her new neighbours.

When she becomes romantically involved with her boss, she can't believe her luck. But things are about to take a grisly turn.

As her colleagues and neighbours are killed off one by one, Hannah's idyllic life starts to fall apart. But when her mother becomes the next victim, the connection to Hannah is all too real.

Who is watching her every move?

Will the police discover the real killer in time?

Hannah is about to learn that appearances can be deceptive.

Do you love **gripping psychological thrillers** full of twists and turns? If so you'll love **best-selling** author Netta Newbound's stunning new *Maggie*.

When sixteen-year-old Maggie Simms' mum loses her battle with cancer, the only family she has left is her **abusive stepfather**, Kenny.

Horrified to discover he intends to continue his nightly abuse, Maggie is **driven to put a stop to him once and for all**.

However, she **finds her troubles are only just beginning** when several of her closest allies are killed.

Although nothing seems to be linking the deaths, Maggie believes she is jinxed.

Why are the people she cares about being targeted?

And who is really behind the murders?

Sometimes the truth is closer than you think.

Victoria and Jonathan Lyons seem to have everything—a perfect marriage, a beautiful daughter, Emily, and a successful business. Until they discover Emily, aged five, has a rare and fatal illness.

Medical trials show that a temporary fix would be to transplant a hormone from a living donor. However in the trials the donors die within twenty four hours. Victoria and Jonathan are forced to accept that their daughter is going to die.

In an unfortunate twist of fate Jonathan is suddenly killed in a farming accident and Victoria turns to her sick father-in-law, Frank, for help. Then a series of events present Victoria and Frank with a situation that, although illegal, could save Emily.

Will they take their one chance and should they?

An Edge of your Seat Psychological Thriller Novella

All her life twenty-two-year-old Ruby Fitzroy's annoyingly over protective mother has believed the worst will befall one of her two daughters. Sick and tired of living in fear, Ruby arranges a date without her mother's knowledge.

On first impressions, charming and sensitive Cody Strong seems perfect. When they visit his home overlooking the Welsh coast, she meets his delightful father Steve and brother Kyle. But it isn't long before she discovers all is not as it seems.

After a shocking turn of events, Ruby's world is blown apart. Terrified and desperate, she prepares to face her darkest hour yet.

Will she ever escape this nightmare?

ABOUT THE AUTHOR

My name's Netta Newbound. I write thrillers in many different styles — some grittier than others. The Cold Case Files have a slightly lighter tone. I also write a series set in London, which features one of my favourite characters, Detective Adam Stanley. My standalone books, The Watcher, Maggie, My Sister's Daughter and An Impossible Dilemma, are not for the faint hearted, and it seems you either love them or hate them—I'd love to know what you think.

If you would like to be informed when my new books are released, visit my website: www.nettanewbound.com and sign up for the newsletter.

This is a PRIVATE list and I promise you I will only send emails when a new book is released or a book goes on sale.

If you would like to get in touch, you can contact me via Facebook or Twitter. I'd love to hear from you and try to respond to everyone.

facebook.com/newboundnetta
twitter.com/nettanewbound

ACKNOWLEDGMENTS

There are so many wonderful people who deserve thanks and praise for supporting me through every process of my writing - from the initial idea, through to the final polishing I couldn't do it without each and every one of you. To my girlies - Susan, Sandra, Jules, Sheryl and Serena - you keep me sane. To Gloria, Kristina, Shelly, Susan F, Sharon, Donna, Emma, Gaynor, and all the people behind the scenes at Junction Publishing who work tirelessly to get the word out there. To Marco - my wonderful friend and colleague. To my fabulous readers who spur me on all the time. To Marika and Ross - you rock. And last, but definitely not least, my family who mean the absolute world to me. From the bottom of my heart — thank you xxx

Printed in Great Britain
by Amazon